W9-CBB-689

JOLLOF RICE
AND OTHER
REVOLUTIONS

JOLLOF RICE AND OTHER REVOLUTIONS

A NOVEL IN INTERLOCKING STORIES

OMOLOLA IJEOMA OGUNYEMI

AMISTAD

An Imprint of HarperCollins*Publishers*

Early versions of the following stories in *Jollof Rice and Other Revolutions* were previously published: "Fodo's Better Half," *Farafina*, Issue 8, January 2007; "Area Boy Rescue," in *New Writing From Africa 2009*, Johnson and KingJames Books, 2009; "Reflections from the Hood of a Car," *Camera Obscura Journal of Literature and Photography*, Volume 5, 2012; "Jollof Rice and Revolutions," *Ploughshares*, 2017, 43(2):192–204.

HarperCollins books may be purchased for educational, business, or sales promotional use. For information, please email the Special Markets Department at SPsales@harpercollins.com.

FIRST EDITION

Design by Nancy Singer

Library of Congress Cataloging-in-Publication Data has been applied for.

ISBN 978-0-06-311704-4

22 23 24 25 26   LSC   10 9 8 7 6 5 4 3 2 1

Para Alejandro con todo mi corazón.

Each new generation begins with nothing and with everything. They know all the earlier mistakes. They may not know that they know, but they do.

—Ben Okri, *The Famished Road*

CONTENTS

JOLLOF RICE
AND OTHER
REVOLUTIONS

FODO'S BETTER HALF

1897–1931

ADAOMA

On a clear February morning in 1897, as British forces sacked Benin City, Monye's wife went into labor. Monye and his wife lived in the town of Anioma-Ukwu, which, heading east, was a morning's walk to the River Niger, and heading west, an eight-hour walk to the Kingdom of Benin. Forty-eight hours after her water broke, the Kingdom of Benin was a pile of smoking ruins, and Monye's wife was dead.

A few hours after their daughter was born, Monye's wife smiled weakly at her husband, saying, "She is so beautiful, *ada oma*." She gasped a little. "I'm tired, I need to sleep. Please promise me that you will take good care of her."

"Of course I will. . . . We will," said Monye. "We'll both take good care of Adaoma together. Just get some rest and build up your strength." He reached his hand out and gently held her right hand, trying to keep the panic coursing through his body out of his voice. The midwife had told him that she'd lost too much blood.

His wife gripped his hand for a few seconds and then let go. Closing her eyes, she drifted off to sleep. She never woke up.

―――――

Monye had made a small fortune from a handful of cows, a sizable number of goats, and an oil-palm plantation. None of this was a consolation in the wake of his wife's passing. Friends urged him to send the baby away as a bearer of bad luck, but Monye couldn't exile his wife's face, her smile. His sister was still with milk for her eighteen-month-old son and became her niece's wet nurse, strapping Adaoma to her back as she carried out her daily chores. Despite long hours of hard work, Monye found time to play with his daughter every day, marveling at her soft skin, her dimples, the way she grabbed her heels and gummed her toes when she was hungry, instead of crying. She was a reincarnation of the woman who pushed her out, the only reminder left to him, and he so wanted to remember. Two new wives and seven more children, five boys and two girls, did little to diminish the memory of his first wife, the near-worship of his first child.

———

The first time Adaoma got married, Monye made sure the world knew he was parting with a jewel.

Adaoma spied Onochie, her future husband, at her very first egwu onwa outing in Anioma-Ukwu, a few months after her fourteenth birthday. Her little brothers and sisters had been put to bed—they trailed her everywhere she went when they were awake. The moon was almost dazzling in its brilliance as she skipped from her father's compound of mud-walled homes to the community square to meet her best friend, Mgbolie. Mgbolie was half a year older and had been going to egwu onwa for over three months, but Adaoma was not allowed to join the monthly, moonlit gathering of young people because she was not yet of age; her period hadn't made an appearance until now. She had prayed daily for it to arrive and when it finally did, she ran, overjoyed, to find Mgbolie.

"It has finally come!"

Mgbolie understood immediately. She jumped up and clapped. "Somebody will be singing at egwu onwa soon." Then she grabbed Adaoma's hands and improvised a little dance.

As Adaoma walked toward the gathering area, a night breeze stirred, bringing down the temperature from what had been a scorching hot day. Her spirit was buoyed by the sounds of crickets chirping and toads croaking and she started to hum. She always felt inspired by nature, hearing music in the rustle of the trees and the gurgle of water from streams; she would belt out whatever tune came to her mind hearing those notes. The moon illuminated the way; no need for a palm-oil lamp to guide her. She felt all grown up; Anioma-Ukwu people rose and went to bed with the rising and setting of the sun. Without the arrival of her period and egwu onwa, she would have been asleep by now.

———

Adaoma observed the throng of young people in the sandy square, girls mostly in the left half of the square in short and mid-length off-white casual wrappers, some tied at the waist, some under the breasts, some over their breasts, depending on whether they were planning to dance or sing for the gathering. In the right half of the square, the boys chatted, their waist-to-knee-length npes tied in knots at the waist so that even the most energetic dances couldn't pry them loose.

Mgbolie was deep in conversation with another girl, so Adaoma snuck up behind her, placing her hands over Mgbolie's eyes.

"Adaoma," Mgbolie said. "I know it's you—you're the only one who does that." She turned around to look at her friend. "I'm so happy you're finally here."

Adaoma laughed and hugged her friend, eyes still wide as she took in the scene.

4

"What are you going to do?" she asked Mgbolie.

"Obiageli and I are planning to sing—you can join us."

Adaoma had a great voice and had never been known for her shyness.

As she cast her eyes about the square, they lingered over a tall, slim brown-skinned boy, about five years older than her. His eyes locked with hers for a moment and then he looked down at the ground as if confused. Adaoma kept her eyes on him, waiting to see if he would look up again. He didn't.

"Who's that?" Adaoma pointed toward him delicately with her lips and chin.

Mgbolie looked in the direction indicated. "Him? That's Onochie. Wonderful dancer but he is too shy."

Adaoma didn't think she would have a problem with that.

"Oh, look, Adaoma," Mgbolie said, "I think Chijike is looking at you." Obiageli and Mgbolie giggled.

Adaoma glanced at the young man Mgbolie was pointing out. He was good-looking, slightly bowlegged, with a thick neck. His body rippled with well-defined muscles from farmwork.

"He is handsome," she said. "But I like him better." She turned her head toward Onochie, who had been looking their way. He started at this renewed attention and cast his eyes back down.

"You're crazy," said Obiageli. "That one doesn't know how to speak to anything but his feet. Chijike is not like that at all."

"That's okay," said Adaoma. "I'll get Onochie to speak to me."

———

Adaoma got her chance a month later. She had walked to Mgbolie's house and they both strolled to egwu onwa together. After greeting many of the other girls gathered, they were debating which songs to sing when Mgbolie said, "Guess who's watching you?"

Adaoma looked up in time to catch Onochie staring in her direction. The moment he saw her looking, he redirected his eyes to his feet.

"I'll be right back," she said to Mgbolie.

She walked around the edges of the crowd, made her way to where Onochie stood, stopped a little ways in front of him, and glued her eyes to his feet. Onochie shifted around a bit in embarrassment but Adaoma didn't break her gaze. After assessing his feet for a good while, she looked up at him and smiled cheekily.

"I'm really disappointed," she said. "I thought for sure you had six or seven toes."

Onochie seemed stunned for a moment and then he cracked up, a joyful, infectious sound. Adaoma sucked in her breath at the beauty of his laugh and then joined in.

"I'm Onochie," he said, as the laughter subsided.

"Of course I know who you are," Adaoma replied. "What's my name?"

"Adaoma." He was gaping at her now, half admiring her boldness, half concerned at what she would say next.

"Good, good, good," she said. "I like the way you say it."

Onochie looked at no other girl from that day on.

―――――

By the time Adaoma was fifteen and Onochie twenty, Onochie's family had expressed their interest in Adaoma to Monye. Onochie worked hard at the plots of land his father gave him, growing cassava, yams, and other crops that would help build their life together. Monye's scouts reported back favorably about Onochie's farm. He then asked Adaoma what she thought of Onochie. After the conversation with Adaoma, he was satisfied that his daughter would be happy and in good hands. When Onochie's family came knocking on Monye's door, they were warmly received.

Monye commissioned Anioma-Ukwu's best weaver to make five akwaocha, brilliant white wrappers with intricate and unique red designs at the borders for Adaoma's wedding outfit and trousseau.

On the day of the wedding, Adaoma's aunt and stepmothers fussed over her, rubbing nzu over her flawless, oval face and lining her almond-shaped eyes with otanjele.

Her stomach roiled from the excitement; she hadn't been able to eat much of anything offered to her.

"You will faint if you don't eat something," one of her step-mothers said. "And then people will start to wonder . . ."

Adaoma choked down half a slice of yam after hearing this but couldn't take any more than that. She said, "I will eat after I see my husband."

The women joked as they prepped her. "So you can't eat anymore if you don't see Onochie?"

"Hmm, you will starve when he goes to the farm oh."

"God forbid that he has to travel to Onitsha or Igbuzo to sell something. What will become of you then?"

"Don't mind them, Adaoma. I couldn't eat on my wedding day either. I looked like a stick that day but look at how nice and round I am now."

They teased her and one another and laughed until Adaoma joined in and was finally able to ignore her unsettled stomach.

She tied an akwaocha with red drum patterns at the border, her hair braided on top of her head into a crown of deep red coral beads that echoed the red designs on her wrapper. She had a matching coral bead necklace, earrings, and bracelets on each wrist.

Two cows, twenty chickens, and seven goats had been slaughtered to prepare a feast, because Monye wanted to be sure that there was enough for guests to gorge until they were sick with food.

Onochie sat facing the elders who had gathered to bless the ceremony, an empty wooden chair beside him, members of his extended family seated to his left in their whitest akwaocha. Adaoma's extended family was seated to his right, facing his family, with the exception of her stepmothers and the handful of female relatives helping to get her ready.

Four of Adaoma's unmarried female cousins were sent out to Onochie, one after the other, with large pieces of cloth draped over their heads. They were sent back as Onochie shook his head each time. "She is not my bride."

When Adaoma finally emerged to stand by Onochie's side for the elders' blessings, the women attending the wedding gasped. Her face was perfect, her ebony skin glowing in beautiful contrast to the white wrapper she wore. The coral jewelry was striking, gleaming bright red against her dark skin. Women smiled and murmured to one another approvingly. Coral in that deep red shade was almost impossible to find.

"Ah, Monye tried," one woman said to her friend. "I have never seen coral so expensive, but it is only fitting for a bride as gorgeous as she is."

After the kola nut and palm wine were blessed and shared between the two families, the gifts from the groom's family presented, and the festivities, eating, and dancing ended, it was time for Adaoma to be taken to her husband's home. Her sisters and unmarried young cousins led the way, carrying Adaoma's trousseau and belongings for her new life. The procession made its way slowly from Monye's compound at dusk, with passersby stopping to stare at the bride and the items on display.

There were five hand-woven white wrappers for special occasions draped artfully in a wooden chest to show off the red decorations at their borders; five plainer off-white wrappers for everyday wear in another wooden chest; a large mortar and pestle for pounding yam; a flat mortar and pestle for grinding pepper; two enormous three-legged iron pots, a rarity in a town where most only had access to clay cooking pots; two smaller clay cooking pots; a huge clay pot for storing cool drinking water; wooden plates and bowls; four decorative jute mats; two wooden stools; three small carved boxes, each filled with a set of coral bead earrings, necklaces, and bracelets ranging from pinkish red to dark red in hue. Four of Adaoma's young male cousins struggled at the rear of the procession with the largest item, a carved ebony bed that epitomized luxury in a town where most slept on mats or black-stained earthen platforms.

Anioma-Ukwu townspeople told stories about Adaoma's wedding for years after the event, each story increasing the number of cows, goats, and chickens eaten, the number of guests fed, and the belongings she took to her husband's home, until everyone was convinced that the procession was half the length of the town, with twice the number of items she had actually received from her father.

———

Onochie was a light sleeper and he woke up first almost every morning. He would lean over Adaoma and drink in her face, smiling until the intensity of his gaze made her stir and smile back. Sometimes he tickled her feet lightly to wake her up and she slapped at her feet until she realized what was going on and got up groggily.

"Stop that! I always think a mouse is nibbling my toes."

On cooler harmattan mornings, he would sometimes get up and make akamu for both of them in the kitchen at the back of their mud-brick home. A faint smoky odor of food and wood burning would wake her up and she'd stay in bed until he was done.

"I'd be proclaimed the worst wife in Anioma-Ukwu if your mother could see you stirring that pot," she'd say.

"Well, if that makes me the best husband, I'm fine with that," he'd tease.

He usually headed out to his farm after the third cock crow.

Every morning, after he left, Adaoma worked on the little garden behind their home, planting or harvesting different greens and peppers or weeding. Once a week, she'd go to her father's place to fetch her little sisters and cornrow their hair. They wouldn't allow anyone else to do it; she had the perfect combination of a light touch and a flair for style that no one else seemed to be able to match. After gardening or braiding, Adaoma would hurry into the storeroom and arrange piles of smoked fish and other goods that she planned to sell in the marketplace. She'd discovered that she was very good at convincing people to buy things and was starting to gain a reputation as a savvy businesswoman. She spent most of her days preparing food items to sell or actually selling them in the marketplace on Afor days. Before dusk, she would rush home to cook, always anticipating what Onochie would like to eat that day, and as they ate she would tell him all about her day, who had tried to cheat her and what she did about it, and he'd talk about how well the farm was doing or the large snakes, deer, antelope, porcupine, or snails he and his helpers had found. There was always laughter ringing out from their home; it made people smile as they walked by.

———

After Adaoma's marriage entered its second year, her mother-in-law came to visit. The woman's face was a leathery map of misery, lines etched so deep into her forehead that she looked elderly even though she was barely forty.

"Mama, what is wrong?" Adaoma asked, after offering food and water and being turned down for both with an impatient flick of the hand.

"What is not wrong, Adaoma? What is not wrong? What have you done?" Her mother-in-law got up from her chair and paced back and forth, cracking the knuckles of her right hand and then those on the left.

"Mama, what do you mean?" She had a good idea where this was going but refused to make it any easier for her mother-in-law. Adaoma was direct in all things and her love for Onochie had overflowed into everything—she had embraced his mother eagerly in the first few months of marriage, cooking for her, going to the market, fetching water, bringing her gifts. She'd slowly come to the realization that the strange looks, weak and unpaid compliments, odd silences where there should have been thank-yous, were signs that her new mother-in-law did not share her affection. There were never any harsh words spoken in those months, just coldness and a lack of reciprocity. She retreated then, keeping her fears about not getting pregnant to herself, her aunt, and Mgbolie. She had reached the point where she rolled herself into a ball of agony each time her period arrived. Mgbolie was married a few months after her but already had a baby girl. Adaoma's aunt took her to herbalists who gave her one concoction after another to drink, but nothing seemed to work.

"Your womb is locked up and, as if that's not bad enough, you have locked up my son's brains, too." The woman began to sniffle, fat tears sliding down her face and plopping onto her wrapper. "Please have mercy on me. I have only one son, do not expose my shame."

Adaoma felt a piercing pain in her chest. She jumped up

to leave the room, not wanting the older woman to see her tears. Onochie's mother was too quick, though. She ran and faced Adaoma, blocking her access to the doorway. Then she grabbed Adaoma's waist and held on, crying all the while. "Adaoma, if you have ever felt anything for him, if you want what's good for him, please allow him to have children. Please. I'm begging you. He won't listen to anything I say so it's you that I'm begging. Please."

Adaoma stood with her head bowed. "Mama, I know something must be done. Of course he will have children. Don't worry," she said. Her voice was soft, each syllable an unspilled tear. "Don't worry."

Later that day, she went to visit Mgbolie, the bare bones of a plan worked out. She would handpick a new wife for Onochie, someone she could get along with and who looked like she would bear children.

Mgbolie listened to Adaoma's idea without interrupting, then said, "Why don't you wait a little longer? What does that old yam-head know anyway? People say it took her many years to have Onochie. It could be the same thing for you."

Adaoma shook her head. "She was a second wife, she wasn't in the same position as me. Mgbolie, trouble is coming from my in-laws. Big trouble. And all my father's influence will not help me with this one. I have to do something now."

Mgbolie started to say something but there was a closed-off look on Adaoma's face that let her know her friend's mind was made up.

———

Adaoma went home and cooked Onochie's favorite dish, awai, throwing into a pot huge chunks of yam, bits of plantain, greens, dried shrimp, fresh and smoked fish. She smiled as he wolfed down his food and picked at hers. Finally he paused, noticing that she didn't have her usual appetite.

"Are you feeling okay?"

"I'm well," she said. "It's just that I've been thinking about something."

He stopped eating, looking worried. "What is it?"

"We don't have any children and it has been two years now. I think it is time to find a co-wife."

"That is a bad idea," Onochie said. "Children take time sometimes. I mean, I grew up hearing that it took my mother three years to have *me*."

"I know," Adaoma said. "But I really think that this would help."

Onochie shook his head no, and continued eating, slowly now, chewing each bit of food carefully, his mind deep in thought. "Adaoma, I don't think this is necessary." He shook his head again.

It took another year and a half of convincing for Onochie

to agree to the arrangement, but in the end, he did, on the condition that she'd pick their new wife. Adaoma settled on a young woman, Udoka, who lived on the outskirts of the town. She seemed nice, eager to please, and happy to be a co-wife. Four months after Adaoma's first visit with her family, Udoka and Onochie were married.

Udoka gave birth to four children in quick succession, two boys and two girls. Onochie's mother was overjoyed and quickly made it clear that Udoka was her favorite daughter-in-law. To his mother's surprise, however, Onochie paid more attention to Adaoma than to Udoka. They had become almost of one mind in their first three and a half years of marriage. He was secretly relieved that Adaoma had been the one to address their childlessness head-on and to propose what to do about it. While he was grateful to Udoka for the fact that he now had children, he loved Adaoma and trusted her judgment and business sense, something his mother could not understand, because she had never known that in her marriage.

———

Five years after their new wife joined them, her oldest son fell ill with stomach pangs. After a day of whispering with her mother-in-law, Adaoma's co-wife accused her of poisoning the boy. Adaoma couldn't believe it. She loved her husband's children as though she had carried them herself, and lavished them with gifts, braiding the little girls' hair the way she braided her own sisters'. Onochie dismissed Udoka's ramblings initially, but after a few days, Adaoma saw a shadow of doubt cross his face and knew things would never again be as they once were. The boy recovered, but an odor of distrust and paranoia had engulfed their home. Udoka's nostrils flared slightly whenever she saw Adaoma and she tried to keep the children from going to "Big Mother," their name for her. The hair braiding sessions continued only because the girls would scream and cry if anyone else tried to make their hair. This only made things worse with Udoka.

One day, while Adaoma was cooking, two of her stepdaughters came by the kitchen and stared at the pot of fish stew she was making with such large eyes that she broke off little chunks of fish for them, and they ran off squealing with delight.

Soon after, Udoka burst into the kitchen and screamed, "Leave my children alone, you barren witch!"

Adaoma stepped away from the pot she'd been stirring, a coldness spreading down her spine and leaving gooseflesh on her skin at the words she'd just heard. "Are you mad?" she said. "There is something seriously wrong with you and you need to leave the kitchen right now."

"What are you going to do if I don't leave? Exactly what are you going to do?" Udoka stared at her for a good while, eyes blazing with hatred.

Adaoma's hand went up involuntarily to her throat; she

had never felt afraid of Udoka before, but at this moment, she did.

The gesture set Udoka off and she picked up a spoon, striking Adaoma with the edge of it. The blow was hard enough to leave a small gash under Adaoma's left cheek.

Adaoma's brain unfroze. She grabbed the spoon from Udoka, pushed her down onto the kitchen floor, sat on her, and pummeled Udoka until she started to yell, "She's killing me. She's going to kill me."

The children ran into the kitchen, the oldest boy tugging at Adaoma's waist to pull her off his mother.

"Big Mother, please stop, please stop," he screamed.

Adaoma felt a fog lift from her and she looked around. Her hands, face, and sides hurt, and there was warm blood sliding down her left cheek and leaving deep red dots on Udoka's off-white wrapper. Udoka moaned, half passed out. Her lower lip was swollen and there was a greenish contusion on her forehead. The children were crying uncontrollably, their little faces contorted with shock and fear. Adaoma saw with clarity what her life in this home would become; a series of petty battles fought with an alarming ferocity that would bruise her soul and make her feel bone-weary and dejected. Onochie was a quiet, proud man who hated the kind of disruption that was now almost a monthly occurrence in their home. He could have a life of peace surrounded by the children he had always wanted and now had, but Adaoma knew there would never be sanity as long as she and Udoka were in the same space. Udoka's fear was elemental, stoked and enlarged by Onochie's preference for his first wife, no matter how many children Udoka had for him, how well she cooked, how she tried to please him, how much his mother adored her. And her mind had worked and worked until she came to the conclusion that the reason he didn't fully see her was that Adaoma had some unnatural hold on him, an evil that had to be broken. She'd jumped to the conclusion that Adaoma had poisoned her son but his recovery made her no less paranoid—she was essentially fighting for her survival and that of her children. That would not change. Adaoma saw this now. She decided that it was on her to make things whole, and she knew she had to get started before Onochie returned home from the farm.

She hugged the children one by one as Udoka looked on, too dazed to protest. Then she gathered up her clothes and jewelry and went to see her father.

"Enyi mba, zogbu ajahu," she said. This was the greeting for the men of his family. She usually loved saying it; the words filled her head with images of regal elephants trampling unworthy fools, cowards, and traitors. She stayed silent after greeting him, trying to put together the words that would end her marriage.

"What is that on your face?" Monye asked, pointing at the gash on her cheek. "Did Onochie do this to you?" His voice rose in anger.

"No, it wasn't him," Adaoma said. "But it is time for me to go."

She gave her father a short version of events since her stepson fell ill, and asked him to bless her moving on. He looked at his daughter carefully for a long time. She winced as he touched his hand to her left cheek. There was a sheen in his eyes. "No father wants to see his child miserable," he said. "But is this really the way to deal with the issue? Why not let Onochie decide what he wants to do?"

"I have thought it through. It is the hardest thing I've ever had to do but I know it's the right thing." Her face was set, stubborn. He knew that look well.

As Adaoma had requested, Monye sent back the bride price, and with that, her marriage to Onochie was over. Monye gathered some trusted workers together to build Adaoma a new home with a large plot of land next to his compound.

————

After leaving Onochie's house, Adaoma avoided contact with him by going to stay for five months with a relative in Onitsha to learn more about trading in smoked fish, salt, and other goods. Eventually, she was able to numb her mind so that the ache she felt when her thoughts went to him grew duller and duller, until there was just a low-level, constant pain that was bearable, that became normal. She threw herself into growing her trade when she returned to Anioma-Ukwu. With some money that her father gave her, Adaoma expanded her smoked fish business and branched into hand-woven cloth, which was sought after as far away as Onitsha.

Onochie didn't come to look for her. He had tried to find out where she was from her relatives while she was away and finally given up, understanding that her mind was made up and resenting her for making such a consequential decision without first speaking with him. One day in the marketplace, Adaoma spotted Udoka and one of her daughters. Udoka had been very careful not to be in the same place as Adaoma since the beating. But she couldn't prevent her four-year-old from running up to Adaoma.

"Big Mother," she said, smiling. "Where did you go?"

Adaoma hugged the little girl and took her back to her mother, who stood frozen, her features distorted with fright. Udoka looked terrible. She'd lost weight and her round prettiness had given way to a haggard look.

"Thank you," she said in a fearful whisper, as Adaoma handed the child over. Then she walked away as quickly as she could. That day, instead of heading home after the market closed, Adaoma made her way to Mgbolie's. She was barely through the door when she broke down and started to weep, her body quivering, vibrating with each exhalation. Mgbolie hugged her, and, after a few minutes, began to sob herself.

Through tears, Adaoma told Mgbolie that she now realized what she wanted most—a family of her own, children to care for and dote on, who would look after her in her old age.

————

Within five years of leaving Onochie, Adaoma had made enough money from her smoked fish, salt, and cloth trade to be a chief in her own right. She had constant discussions with Mgbolie about the business and how well it was going, but how she would exchange all of it for a child of her own.

One day, Mgbolie stopped by to visit Adaoma, who thought it odd that she had come alone; she usually brought her children with her and Adaoma braided their hair, or cooked something special for them to eat, with the smallest child strapped to her back, dancing as she worked to lull the baby to sleep.

"Is everything okay?" Adaoma searched Mgbolie's face for any signs of bad news but she looked almost serene.

Mgbolie smiled but said nothing for a few moments. Then, "You know my cousin Okafor?"

"No," said Adaoma. "Which cousin is that?"

"My great-uncle's grandson. He has a farm but he developed too much of a taste for palm wine after his crops failed and owes a lot of people money."

Adaoma slapped at her leg, catching an early evening mosquito mid-bite and scraping its smashed remains off her palm.

"That's a shame really," she said. "Where are my children? Why didn't you bring them?"

Mgbolie ignored the questions, continuing her Okafor story. "Okafor's oldest daughter is Fodonika. You know her, Fodo, very skinny, with knock-knees. Her mother sends her to the market to buy fish sometimes and she asks to pay in installments."

Adaoma knew then who Mgbolie was talking about. "Oh yes, I know her. Tiny girl. Always polite."

"Fodo has liked this boy Imma since they met at egwu onwa, and they want to get married," Mgbolie continued. "The thing is Imma's family has no money, and Okafor needs a lot, so he is planning to marry Fodo off to Chief Udeze as his fourth wife."

Adaoma was aghast. "But the man is so old!"

"Yes oh. That's how it is." Mgbolie gazed at Adaoma intently. She spoke slowly, carefully. "But this could be your opportunity. You have as much wealth as Udeze. And it would be a better outcome for Fodo."

Adaoma parsed Mgbolie's words, a mixture of hope and elation bubbling up in her as she slowly grasped what Mgbolie was suggesting. She made enough to support a family, could afford whatever bride price Fodo's father wanted. Fodo would still be able to see Imma, and Adaoma could have the family she wanted through the young couple's love. Still, she hesitated, speaking more to herself than to Mgbolie. "When Akunna married that girl—what's her name now?—her father had no sons so it was understood that their children would carry on his name and his line."

"But Akunna is not the only example. That's not the only reason. You have proven that you can support a family. It's time for you to have one."

Adaoma rubbed the raised scar on her cheek with her little finger, an unconscious gesture she now made when she was uncertain but intrigued by something. She composed her face, trying to still the rush of exhilaration that was making her heart beat faster. This felt like a solution. It could be. But what if Fodo didn't agree—she was sure the father would go for it but Fodo might have strong opinions of her own. Then what? She tried to swat down the whole idea by raising a different concern. "But Fodo is so bony. There are boys with larger breasts than hers. How am I sure she'll be able to have children?"

Mgbolie laughed. "Nothing can be known until it is tried. I wouldn't judge by the way she looks."

"Of course, of course." Adaoma got up, a smile rearranging the placid mask she'd trained her face to assume in the wake of her failed marriage. "Thank you, Mgbolie." She hugged her friend tight until Mgbolie mock-complained that she might soon be dead because she couldn't breathe. Adaoma let go, but couldn't keep her hands still, clapping them together softly, like a small child. "Excuse me," she said finally, "I have to go talk to my father."

Mgbolie smiled. "I'll walk with you to the ube tree."

———

Adaoma's wedding to Fodo in 1927 was a small, low-key affair. The only thing Fodo's father had in abundance was talk; Adaoma had to send him enough to cover the wedding feast so that shame would not come to both families when the guests arrived. Fodo's father gave her exactly five items for her trousseau: a special-occasion akwaocha, another for casual wear, a clay cooking pot, a mat, and an Igbo Bible.

Fodo was grateful for the fact that she could see Imma as much as she wanted, that she would be encouraged to do so, in fact. Imma had resigned himself to losing her to an old man, so he was relieved that he could still be with her even though his children would carry another's name and be recognized by everyone in town as Adaoma's.

Adaoma and Fodo's marriage was a happy one at first. When Fodo gave birth to their son, Uchenna, in 1928, Adaoma danced and cried as the midwife held the boy out to her. She made fish peppersoup, spooning the fragrant broth and chunks of fish into Fodo's mouth, worried at how weakened she was from childbirth. A month after Uchenna was born, Adaoma was braiding Fodo's hair as the boy slept soundly on her back. She could feel his tiny heartbeat against her skin and the faint but steady drumbeat made her almost want to weep with joy.

"My father's servant just got back from Onitsha," she said. "I sent him there to find something a while ago, but it took him some time to get it."

"What is it?" Fodo shifted as she sat to get more comfortable; she still wasn't completely free of pain but was feeling much stronger now.

"Let me show you." Adaoma went into the storeroom and emerged with two wooden boxes, which she presented to Fodo.

Fodo opened the first one. It had a full set of deep red coral bead jewelry. The second had an even more striking set, deeper red than the first. She gasped. "This must have cost a fortune!"

"Nothing is too expensive for the mother of my child," Adaoma said. She grinned widely as she took in Fodo's awed reaction. "You have made me so happy; and I will do all that I can to make you happy."

She went back to braiding Fodo's hair. "Why don't you read to me from that book of yours?"

Fodo had gone to the new mission school in Anioma-Ukwu for a few years before her father fell on hard times and turned to drink. Adaoma was proud of the fact that Fodo could read and would often have her read aloud from the Igbo Bible she'd brought with her. While she didn't care much for the religion that Fodo had adopted, she thought the book was entertaining, with some of the craziest stories she had ever heard.

———

"He looks so much like you, Vero," Imma said, cradling a five-month-old Uchenna in his arms as he examined him by the light of a black clay palm-oil lamp. "Handsome boy. He's so healthy . . . and fat—just look at those cheeks!"

Fodo laughed. "He takes after his father," she teased. "He can eat! Oh my God, I was drinking akamu yesterday—he would watch the spoon going into my mouth and swallow when I swallowed, so I started to feel guilty, the way he was staring at me with drool at the sides of his mouth. I'd already breast-fed him but I thought, 'I'll give him a little bit of akamu, just to taste.'" She traced a finger across the sleeping Uchenna's lips. He pursed them and turned his head away from her without waking. "Imma, would you believe that he held my hand and kept eating until he finished all my akamu! He was sweating and dancing and happy, smacking his lips. I was so shocked."

Imma laughed out loud. "He is truly an Okolo! We've never met food we didn't like."

They both shivered in the awkward pause after the words tumbled out of his mouth. Uchenna was definitely not an Okolo. At least not in Anioma-Ukwu. He was Adaoma's son, a Nwajei, and would never answer to Imma's last name, never have an acknowledged relationship with his biological father, no matter how much Imma might want differently.

Adaoma was in Onitsha for two days on a business trip and so Fodo had made her way to Imma's family's compound just after dusk with Uchenna. She planned to head back home just before dawn with the baby so that Adaoma wouldn't find out. Adaoma would hate to know that Fodo had taken her son to Imma's.

"You know, every day I pray," Imma said. "I think about this life and I pray. I pray that one day, you and I will get married in the church. We'll be Immanuel and Veronica Okolo, and nothing anyone can say or do will separate us."

"Imma, stop it. If not for Adaoma I would be Udeze's wife and this would not be your boy." Fodo felt the tears catch in the back of her throat. "I know what you mean, but this is the life that found us."

"I felt indebted to Adaoma at first, but now I don't know," said Imma. "This doesn't have to be our life forever, Vero. There has to be something better for you than being married to someone just because she wants children and is richer than Udeze. I'm still going to school. Teacher says I'm the best student in standard four and I may be able to get an office job!" He nuzzled Uchenna's cheek with his nose. The baby slept on. "Do you know how much a court clerk gets paid?"

"How much?"

"Two pounds a year!"

Fodo sucked in her breath. A goat cost two shillings. With a steady income of two pounds a year, they could live comfortably. "Imma, you know that there's no way that can happen. Unless something happens to Adaoma. She's only been good to me—I wish her no harm."

"I don't wish her harm either, Vero. You know that. I'm just saying that I will keep praying; I'm never going to give up hope." He laid the baby down on an earthen platform piled high with soft cloths and gathered Fodo in his arms. "Have faith; God will make it happen. I don't know how, but I will keep praying."

"I will pray too," Fodo said, nodding.

———

Fodo went to church regularly and tried to get Adaoma to join her, but Adaoma mostly refused. One day, two and a half years after Uchenna was born, she came home and let Adaoma know that there was a new church father, one who looked like them.

"They say he's been to the white man's country and back on a boat," Fodo said, with a tone of wonder.

"Really? A church Fada who looks like you and me?"

"Yes. He speaks a very funny Igbo—we used to almost laugh in the beginning when he would speak, but now we're all used to it. He is a very wise and educated man."

Adaoma wasn't so easily impressed but agreed to come

to the church to hear him preach. The Sunday she attended church, the man nodded to the members of the congregation and greeted Adaoma with the respect deserving of her station as a chief.

Then he climbed up to the pulpit and said, "I want to acknowledge all the women who help to sweep the church every week, especially our sister Veronica, the only person who has never missed even one week. Sister Vero, please stand." He gestured toward Fodo and she stood shyly, head bowed, a proud smile of accomplishment that Adaoma had never before seen covering her face.

The congregation applauded and Adaoma felt a growing sense of unease. She tried to figure out what was bothering her, why she felt out of place. Perhaps it was the fact that she, like most townspeople who hadn't attended the mission school, couldn't say Fodo's name the way the church Fada did: Veronica or Vero. She had attempted it several times but always ended up calling her Fodonika or Fodo. Fodo didn't mind at all, but there was something about the way this man enunciated the syllables of Fodo's name that made Adaoma feel like he sat in a strange world to which she didn't belong, a world filled with knowledge that was hidden from her. Then the man began his sermon. He preached about marriage. About a new way of doing things that left no room for unions like Fodo and Adaoma's.

Adaoma was stunned at what seemed like an ambush. Fodo kept smiling as though all that she was hearing was normal and didn't turn to look Adaoma's way. The church Fada stared directly at Adaoma as he went on, with a smug look that made her want to rush the pulpit screaming and flatten him. Instead, she was careful to keep the mask on her face intact, showing no outward reaction. She had seen what happened to those who tried to prevent new ways of doing things, those who tried to challenge the district officers and the white man's church. Many disappeared and were never heard from again.

She was silent as she walked home with Fodo, filled with a sense of foreboding and wondering why Fodo had asked her to attend the man's sermon. No good could come from what she had heard. A growing fear gripped her and she started to plan. Uchenna was more attached to her than to Fodo; she knew what his every cry meant, knew when to hold him and rock him to sleep and when to ignore him to prevent selfishness from taking root. Fodo had never developed that patience.

A few months after Uchenna's third birthday, Fodo's mother fell ill. Adaoma handed Fodo three pounds in crisp notes, more money than Fodo had ever seen in her life.

"Your mother needs you," she said. "Go take care of her. Uchenna and I will be fine."

Fodo jumped at the opportunity to nurse her mother back to health and help her get the kind of treatment that her father could not afford. She knew Uchenna would be okay, even thought a bit resentfully that he might not notice her absence, given the way he clung to Adaoma every day.

On a cool harmattan morning in 1931, two weeks after Fodo went to take care of her mother, Adaoma slipped out with the boy and a manservant of her father's, a few hours before dawn. She'd laid out her plan to her father and received his blessing. She knew it would be a three-month walk and canoe ride to Lagos, but she had business partners who would host her along the way. She didn't feel bad for Fodo. Imma had also gone to the mission school and had learned enough to gain a sitting-job in the new post office. He didn't have to farm and scrape from the land to sustain a family; with this new way of earning a living, paying a bride price would not be an issue. He'd marry Fodo, they'd start a new family and count their blessings at this new beginning. Adaoma and Uchenna would be safe in Lagos, far from the reach of meddling preachers and their inflexible worldviews. What she didn't count on were recurring nightmares in which she could hear Fodo's loud sobbing in her dreams. The years went on and on, but the crying never stopped.

1938

"Wait. Don't melt. I'm sorry," Fodo gasped. She thrashed about the straw mat, one flailing arm connecting with Imma's face.

Her husband shook her gently. "Vero, wake up. It's just a dream, just a dream. You'll wake the girls."

Slowly, she became aware of her surroundings, taking in

the familiar predawn shadows that defined the sparsely fur-
nished room. On the floor to her right, she made out two
sprawled forms. The sounds of her daughters' even breathing
filled the silence.

Imma pulled Fodo close. Softly kneading the flesh on her
back, he whispered, "You had the dream again."

Fodo shuddered. "This time it was a little different. Adaoma
handed Uchenna to me and I dropped him. I dropped our son.
He shattered like a clay pot into many pieces, and I tried to
gather them up as fast as I could. I knew that if I put them all together he would be fine, but Adaoma started to weep. I'd never
seen her cry before—the tears melted her face as they gushed
from her eyes. She was dissolving right before me, all because
I couldn't save Uchenna. I was trying to tell her to stop, that I
could put him back together, but she kept melting."

Imma held Fodo tighter and shushed her. "Don't worry
yourself so much. It will be okay. It will." After a while, the
gently soothing pressure to her back started to take effect.

Fodo said drowsily, "You're so good to me, Imma. Too
good."

"What does 'too good' mean?" Imma smiled in the dark;
Fodo could hear it in his voice.

She mumbled something he could not decipher and asked,
"What would you like for supper?"

"Beans would be nice." Imma sounded surprised.

"Okay, I'll cook some today." Fodo drifted off to sleep.

———

Fodo's thoughts flitted from one unfinished chore to another as she trudged down the rain-soaked Lagos dirt road. There were tomatoes and peppers to be crushed on the grinding stone for the stew she was going to make, brown beans to be boiled for supper, and the washing to be done once fewer people were using the communal pump. Her store of beans was low, so she had decided to make a trip to the market. Half an hour after she left home, a few rain clouds had suddenly appeared, and though there weren't enough of them to obscure the sun, they let loose a torrent of water. Then, just as abruptly as they had arrived, they raced toward the ocean, leaving the sun to occupy the sky without competition, and bake the mud left behind.

She walked slowly to the market, a small-boned, brown, big-bellied woman with muddy-slippered feet and closely cropped hair covered by a blue-and-yellow scarf. Her blouse was light blue cotton, faded from years of washing. Fastened around it was a blue-and-yellow wrapper cut from the same bale of cloth as the scarf. As she inhaled the subtle fragrance of freshly cleansed earth, Fodo slowed her pace, the list of waiting chores pushed to the back of her mind.

There were stalls displaying huge baskets piled high with bright red tomatoes, peppers, and onions. Fodo barely spared a glance for them as she homed in on the bean seller's stall. Once there, she greeted the bean seller, a heavy, perspiring woman with a three-month-old baby strapped to her back. There was nothing Fodo liked better than to haggle; she had learned how to do it from the best. When the corners of a trader's mouth turned down just a little and fists began to clench, she knew she had cut the profit margin to the barest minimum: it was time to make the purchase. Sellers always shook their heads after an encounter with Fodo, smiling ruefully at their inability to best her. Some no longer bothered to go through the process of haggling. When she approached, they looked around furtively, then spoke in hushed tones: "My last price for this item is . . ." Fodo would stretch out a fist with the whispered amount, confident that she was getting the best possible deal.

The bean seller was not in this group, however.

Pointing at a pyramid of brown beans in a three-foot-wide aluminum bowl, Fodo asked, "How much for six cups?"

"Nah sisi for six cups."

Fodo had exactly eight pence on her and was not about to spend six on beans. "I be good customer now," she said. "Tolo." She watched to see the bean seller's reaction to her halving of the asked price.

The bean seller laughed. "You no want my children to eat today? Okay, bring five pence."

Fodo noticed a flash of bright yellow clothing to her right, just as she was about to counter with an even lower price. At the next row of stalls, she spotted a tall, thin woman with cornrowed hair piled in a bun at the top of her head, and dark, velvety skin, flawless except for a small scar on the left cheek.

"Adaoma!" Fodo yelled out the name, her hands shaking. She clasped her hands to her belly to steady them, hold in the gelatinous goop that now seemed to have replaced her insides.

Adaoma turned quickly toward the sound of Fodo's voice, then darted away down the path between two rows of stalls. Fodo followed, leaving the bewildered bean seller behind.

"Customer, where you dey go?" the woman shouted.

Fodo didn't respond. Although she didn't believe Adaoma would bring him with her to the market, Fodo scanned her surroundings for any sign of Uchenna. The cloth section lay ahead, neatly folded pink, purple, blue, yellow, green, red, and cream lace, dutch-wax, aso-oke, and locally dyed cotton fabrics hanging from wooden racks in stall after stall, stretching for half a mile. Adaoma turned a corner. When Fodo arrived at the same spot, there was no sign of her. She could have ducked into any one of the hundred stalls dotting this part of the market; if she didn't want to be found, there was nothing Fodo could do about it. She held on to a cloth rack to steady herself, inhaling deeply until her body stopped trembling. The cloth seller came out to see whether Fodo wanted to buy something, took a look at her face, and retreated back into the depths of her stall without saying a word. After a few minutes, Fodo walked back to the bean seller, unfastening the edge of her wrapper to reveal three coins, two with large holes at their centers. Fodo handed over the hole-free coin, refastened her wrapper, and took the six cigarette cups of beans. She turned to leave for home without asking for her change.

"Ah," the bean seller said, her head jerking back a little, mouth wide open. "Wait." She handed Fodo a coin with a hole in it and a newspaper sheet folded in the shape of a cone. It was full of extra brown beans. "For my pikin."

Fodo smiled weakly as she accepted the gift for her daughters. "That woman nah someone wey I know before before . . . ," she said. The bean seller nodded sympathetically, though clearly she was still mystified. As she left the bean seller, Fodo's only thought was that her husband would know what to do. They were so close now. Uchenna was probably here in Lagos.

———

Seven years had passed since Fodo had last seen Uchenna. Seven years since Adaoma vanished into the night air with him. Years of inquiry had proved fruitless; the woman and boy had disappeared, leaving no sign that they had ever existed. Maybe she should have yelled out that she just wanted to know that the child was safe. Of course, this would ring false; his safety was never really in question.

In her mind she replayed the two most vivid memories she had of Adaoma and Uchenna. The first took her back to 1930, just two months after the boy's second birthday. He was recovering from a brush with malaria, weakly resisting all Fodo's attempts to feed him by turning his face sharply away from her. Adaoma picked him up and, hugging him to her thin frame, sang one of the nonsensical songs she made up just for him:

Uchenna, you were not born to suffer,
You were not meant to cry
You came to this world to eat laughter
You came to this world to swallow joy
Like pounded yam

At that, he smiled, letting Adaoma feed him small rounded balls of pounded yam dipped in nsala soup with little bits of catfish. When he was done eating, Adaoma sat with her back against the wall, singing a lullaby she'd created on his birthday. He curled himself into her lap and made a pillow of her chest, humming along until they both fell asleep. They looked so peaceful that Fodo left them there, tiptoeing around to avoid waking them.

Her second memory was of Uchenna at three, wailing, inconsolable. Adaoma was at a meeting in the next town; it would be hours until she returned. The boy had wanted to go with her but that was not possible. He waited by the door crying. After an hour Fodo was beyond irritated. She picked him up roughly, rocking him while singing one of Adaoma's lullabies. This just made him sob even louder.

In exasperation, she stuck her left breast in his mouth. He still breast-fed from time to time; usually this shut him up. This time he spat out her nipple, an indignant look on his face. Somehow he knew she was just trying to keep him quiet. He wrested himself from her grasp, jammed his thumb firmly into his mouth, and sat silent, sulking, and determined by the door. Fodo decided to ignore him. When Adaoma finally appeared, his face crinkled into a smile and he clapped his chubby hands together as she scooped him up, the last few hours of crying completely forgotten. Fodo still felt guilty at the white-hot resentment that had coursed through her body, the thought that had crossed her mind then:

"God, why did you give me such a stubborn, annoying child?"

As that memory washed over her, Fodo broke into a jog. She had to get home as soon as possible. Imma would take charge; they would find Adaoma, talk to her and figure out a way to have them all raise Uchenna.

———

Fodo hurried toward the face-me-I-face-you rooms her family shared with six other families. She rushed past the row of mango trees lining the road, getting to the practically deserted communal water pump at the beginning of their street in no time and making her way into the common courtyard.

"Imma," she called, not waiting to get to her family's room before telling her husband, and all her neighbors, proximity being what it was, what had happened at the market. His back was to her as she entered their living area. "I saw Adaoma at the market today and I chased her but she ran into the cloth market and I lost her. At least we now have an idea of where Uchenna is . . ." Fodo's voice trailed off, as she noticed the stranger standing in front of her husband, his hand firmly gripping that of a young boy. A young boy whose lips were a miniature replica of hers.

Her husband turned around looking utterly confused. "You can't have seen Adaoma," he said. He gestured at the stranger. "He came here to fulfill a promise he made Adaoma. She had been sick for some time."

Fodo was still glued to one spot, staring at the son she'd never thought she'd lay eyes on again.

"You can't have seen Adaoma," her husband repeated, "be-cause she died last week."

Fodo felt her knees go weak and sank to the floor. She knew what she had seen: the oval face, the almond eyes, the unmistakable scar on Adaoma's left cheek. Still on her knees, she struggled to move but her legs wouldn't budge. Gathering all her energy, she wobbled unsteadily onto her feet and closed the gap between herself and the boy, clasping her son in an embrace tight enough to choke most of the air from his lungs. As she held him, Fodo half-whispered, half-sang:

"Uchenna, you were not born to suffer,
you were not meant to cry,
you came to this world to eat laughter,
you came to this world to swallow joy,
like pounded yam."

The boy howled then, sobs racking his small frame as Fodo shushed him, rocking back and forth with him in her embrace, oga dinma, oga dinma, it will be okay. Today. Tomorrow. Someday.

JOLLOF RICE AND REVOLUTIONS

1986

REMI

Aisha threw the first stone. The crowd of girls went silent as it arced through the humid twilight, striking the principal's thick ankle. The hush lasted a few seconds more as we processed her gasp. Our principal did feel pain after all. Then Nonso whooped and let a second stone loose.

"Stop!" Mrs. Haastrup shouted and two hundred girls stepped backward. She still had power, the kind that made some girls tie half-slips over their heads before gathering in front of her house to avoid being identified and possibly expelled. But that gasp had strengthened a few girls who stood steady, their faces uncovered. Aisha, Nonso, and I were in that group.

I felt a frisson of spite-filled delight as I watched Mrs. Haastrup clasp her hands to mask her agitation. A few weeks before, she'd berated me in front of the school assembly for wearing a sweater she didn't like with my pinafore, and seized it for not being a dark-enough green. The sweater had been a gift from my aunt for doing exceptionally well in school the previous term. I'd wrapped my arms around my chest, shivering in the harmattan cold, knowing I'd never get my sweater back.

Mrs. Haastrup never seemed interested in how well our studies were going or in rewarding good teachers, never missed an opportunity to humiliate students or her staff in public, eyes dancing with malevolent joy as she took down a fresh victim. An old wooden desk in her office was piled high with a random assortment of items she'd seized from students— blouses, sweaters, scarves, earrings, books, bags, socks, sandals. That desk and the trophies it bore were a symbol of her dominance over our tiny boarding school in Fiditi. The Ministry of Education had sent her a year ago even though she'd made it clear (to them, us, the trees, the grass) that she would have much preferred to head a school in Lagos.

"What do you want?" Mrs. Haastrup asked now, her voice unsteady.

Where should we even begin? I thought about the fired

teachers, the low morale since she took over the job of principal, the fact that her predecessor, Mrs. Adenle, was beloved by students and no one had wanted her to leave. *Respect*, I whispered to myself, remembering the repugnant smell of stale fish stew wafting from her as she'd lectured me about her new school uniform rules. I was one of the best students in my form and generally avoided trouble, but Mrs. Haastrup had reacted as if I'd jumped the fence after hours and headed to a dance with the boys from Faponda Grammar School two miles down the road.

"I said, what do you want?" Mrs. Haastrup let the question drip into the silence that had followed her first asking, her voice stronger now as she sensed our confusion.

"Food," came a voice from the back.

No, not food, I thought, *who was that?* Mrs. Haastrup seized on the word eagerly. "Okay, let's go to the dining hall. I'll ask the cooks to make you some jollof rice." She paused. "With fried meat."

A few of us shouted, "No! Bring back our teachers," but our voices were drowned out by the cries from the crowd: "Fried rice!" "I want asaro."

The crowd surged frantically forward and Mrs. Haastrup laughed. She waved her hand, saying, "Follow me." About sixty girls were left behind in front of the principal's house as the throng moved with her to the dining hall.

Aisha looked from me to Nonso, her mouth gaping.

"Imagine that," she said, when she finally collected herself. She shook her head. "All she had to say was 'jollof rice' and they all forgot what we were here for. We'll never get those teachers back now."

I nodded in disgust, cupped my elbows with my hands, and spat, the memory of stale fish stew overwhelming me. Unable to hold my breath each time Mrs. Haastrup aspirated, I'd thrown up halfway into her school uniform tirade, the thin ogi baba and akara we'd been served for breakfast leaving pink streaks on Mrs. Haastrup's shoes as the assembled girls tittered. My skin sprouted goose bumps as I remembered how cold, small, and nauseated I'd felt.

"Nonso," I said, "what are you thinking?" She was the closest thing we had to an expert on demonstrations and I hoped she knew what to do.

Nonso stayed silent at first. "We didn't have a proper plan," she said finally, looking defeated. "Maybe we should all have agreed on one chant before we got to her house and then she would have known why we were here. Or we should have decided who was going to speak for us." She twisted her right earlobe the way she always did when she was getting agitated. "We shouldn't have let that odensin, that stupid longathroat foodoh, spoil everything."

I reached out and grabbed Nonso's arm with my right hand, Aisha's with my left. "Let's destroy her office. Not everyone can be bought with jollof rice." I spoke loudly so the others could hear me, in a steady voice that didn't match the fluttering in my belly.

We ran from the teachers' living quarters, past the gray-and-yellow art and home economics building with its mural of Nelson and Winnie Mandela. We passed the wooden tuckshop, covered with faded and flaking blue paint, where students bought and sold snacks on weekends and learned about commerce. Soon we got to a large grassy mound with benches and trees where, on visiting days, we met our parents and other family members. The administrative buildings were on the other side of the mound. The rest of the girls followed us from the principal's house, the group swarming like grasshoppers over the grounds that separated the staff quarters from the rest of the school. When we got to the principal's office, I hesitated. I picked up a rock, feeling its weight, liking the sensation of its jagged edges in my palm. I looked behind me at Aisha and Nonso. Aisha was usually the fiery one, the one who got us in all our scrapes, but she was starting to look a bit queasy now. I turned my back on her uneasiness and, lifting my palm, pretended I was practicing the shot put. The shattering of glass louvers made my stomach jump, a tendril of something between fear and joy twisting up my insides. *If my father could see me now, he'd spirit me far, far away from here, never let me speak to any of these girls again.* The rage that followed that thought was sudden and unexpected. I picked up two more stones, walked to the office next to the principal's. Again, there was a satisfying shattering sound. Girls were throwing things all around me. There was glass everywhere and I'd never felt so happy.

———

Nonso lived on the University of Ibadan campus and was full of stories about students rioting—one time when she was in the primary school on campus, the mobile police chased a student into her class, the student bleeding from the head. Her teacher ran to the student and pushed him under her table, screaming at the baton-wielding mobile policeman, *You will not beat him in front of my class*. The policeman stared at her for a while, decided she was crazy or that there were too many witnesses, and left. Nonso said the teacher dropped to her knees afterward, dabbing the student's head with tissue paper from her handbag. Most of her pupils sat still, frozen to their wooden chairs, but Nonso and a few others crawled under the teacher's desk, touching the student's leg, his arm, his neck, trying to soothe him as he groaned in pain.

I looked around for Nonso to see how she was doing. I'd always thought that she wanted to experience her own riot firsthand so she could tell her older brothers how she helped start it and have them gape in awe at her stories for a change. She was sitting on the ground, blouses, sweaters, and scarves from Mrs. Haastrup's trophy table around her, a light trickle of blood flowing from a small cut on her right arm, screeching with laughter and pointing at Mrs. Haastrup's office. "That's what you get when you mess up! That's what you get!" I'd been so busy smashing glass that I hadn't even seen her crawl into the principal's office through the destroyed window.

———

Aisha, Nonso, Solape, and I met on the first day of school four years ago. That day, I clutched my pillow and mosquito net, feeling jittery, as my mother and stepfather walked nervously beside me, carrying my suitcase, broom, cutlass, and hoe. We headed to the school's main assembly area, where we would find out where to go next. A large group of other ten- and eleven-year-old girls stood with their parents, also waiting to hear their dormitory assignments.

Fiditi had been my first-choice school. I was ecstatic when I got the National Common Entrance Exam results and my scores were high enough for any federal boarding school in the country. My mother wanted me to live with her sister in Lagos and attend Queen's College, Yaba, as a day student but I had different plans. I wanted to be a boarder and to be far away from Lagos but not so far that it would be difficult for my parents to visit. Fiditi was ideal, a two-hour drive from my father in Lagos and a one-hour drive from my mother and stepfather in Ibadan. I knew I had to ace the secondary school interviews, so I read the newspapers every day and drew anyone who came near me into discussions about why Indira Gandhi was my hero because I was planning to be the first woman president of Nigeria when I grew up.

"Why not Margaret Thatcher?" my mother said in exasperation one day. "She's a woman too."

"But I don't like her, Mummy," I said.

"That's it?" She rolled her eyes. "Ore mi, you need a much better reason than that."

"I like Indira Gandhi's outfits more than hers," I said, after a little bit of thought.

"Haaaah!" My mother looked shocked and disappointed. "Find out what she's done for her people and what Thatcher has done for hers, then you can talk."

After the interview, I boarded the bus back to Ibadan and pestered my mom and stepfather to find out the results until we learned that I had made it into my first-choice school. And now here we were.

A tall thin woman with a bushy afro and enormous glasses stepped onto the assembly platform in front of the group of parents and new girls. She pulled out a sheet of paper. "Here are the assignments for Queen Amina House. When I call your name, raise your hand, say 'present,' come up the steps with your family, and stand behind me."

I smiled at my mother and whispered, "I want to be in Idia House. Four of the past five head girls have come from Idia House, and I'm going to be head girl by form five."

"Solape Ibironke Orisajimi," said the woman.

"Present." Solape was tiny but had a big booming voice. She was surrounded by her mother, father, and two little boys who I assumed were her younger brothers. She coughed once she was done speaking and then put an inhaler to her mouth, her mom patting her on the back. Her family made their way up to the platform, one brother carrying her pillow and the other her mosquito net while her parents held one end each of a large metal box and Solape gripped the inhaler.

"She has a senior mathset," I said, frowning at my mother. I'd wanted a metal box just like Solape's but my mother had insisted on a leather suitcase and that was that.

"Yours looks much nicer," my mother said.

"Yes, but thieves can cut through leather pretty quickly. No one can break into that thing," I replied.

"Ore mi, God forbid that you be around the kind of people who will slice your suitcase."

I shut up at that.

"Aishatu Maya Danjuma."

"Present," Aisha said. Next to her stood a tall yellow woman with a huge head of curly natural hair, wearing a bright blue caftan. Two aides-de-camp in military uniform were carrying all her school things.

"Her father must be a military man or a government official," my mother mused.

"Chinonso Veronica Ubaka."

Nonso raised her right hand but said nothing.

"Chinonso Veronica Ubaka."

"Oh, I meant 'Present,'" Nonso said, putting her other hand up and wiggling both arms. People started to laugh. She was with two women, a short round one I assumed was her mother and a skinny gray-haired one that had to be her grandmother. They made their way slowly up onto the platform.

"Oluremi Ayoola Adeite."

"Present," I said, shooting my mother a dark look.

"Well, maybe you can be head girl from Queen Amina House," she whispered.

"Not likely. That house has the worst troublemakers in the school, from what I've heard."

"Hmm. Let's go up there before they say you're making trouble already." She pushed me forward.

The woman read eight other names and then we were off to find our new dormitory.

———

Aisha, Nonso, Solape, and I had lived in Queen Amina House for four years. We became friends our first year because I got hazed one evening by Rekia, a senior girl from Ilorin. She'd asked me to fetch water for her from the pump, and I'd brought back a half-full metal bucket.

"What's this?" she'd asked me.

"Your water," I said. "That's how much I could carry."

"But your own bucket is full!"

"My bucket is smaller than yours and since it's plastic, it's lighter. You can have my bucket of water if it bothers you that much or you can fetch your own water next time."

"Heeeee! Who do you think you're talking to like that? Oya, bo si bi." I knew I was in trouble when she switched to Yoruba.

Rekia had me kneel under her bunk bed and fly my arms out to each side to teach me a lesson about mouthing off. Lights-out time arrived and I thought she would ask me to get up, but she didn't. The other seniors said nothing, even though I could sense that they thought she'd gone too far. After a while, my knees hurt, so I stretched out fully on the ground instead of kneeling. Around one a.m., someone shook me gently. It was Aisha, her face weakly illuminated by the one center light left on in the dorm. She put a finger to her lips, pointed at me, and then pointed at her bunk. I couldn't believe she was going to take my place. I whispered, "Thank you," and climbed up to her bed, making sure the mosquito netting was in place so no one could easily tell that it wasn't Aisha. At five thirty, I was shaken awake by Solape; she had her inhaler in her right hand, and when the feel of the hard, cold plastic against my skin startled me, she clapped her left hand over my mouth before I could say anything. She, Nonso, and Aisha had taken turns sleeping under Rekia's bunk so that if Rekia felt under it she'd think I was still there. I lay back down on the floor, and at six when the lights went on and everyone woke, there I was.

The other seniors were horrified to see me curled into a ball underneath the bed. My bunkmate yelled at Rekia, furious. "You mean you didn't let her go to sleep? What kind of a human being are you? I am going to report you to Adenle."

Rekia started to beg because she knew this was potential grounds for suspension or expulsion. She said to me, "Ma binu! I was going to tell you to go back to your bed after an hour; I didn't realize I had fallen so deeply asleep."

I nodded but said nothing. The girls gathered around us gave her disapproving stares. My bunkmate placed a soft, reassuring hand on my neck and smiled at me.

"It was such a small thing," Rekia said. "I was just trying to teach you a little lesson and I fell asleep. Ma binu."

Finally, I said, "Mi o binu," and managed a small smile to show that I truly wasn't angry. She avoided me after that day, no one else tried to haze me (out of sympathy, I thought), and I gained three sisters, so all in all, it was a good deal.

After the Rekia incident, the four of us did everything together and shared our secrets, hopes, and dreams. Solape wanted to be both a lawyer and Nigeria's first astronaut, which we all agreed wasn't a bad goal once we were done laughing. Nonso said, *I hope NEPA isn't in charge of the electricity on your spaceship, because we want to see you return to Earth*. I finally had friends I could talk to about my anger and disappointment that my father didn't want me to live with him after my parents' divorce. Solape said, *I think moms are just better at raising children*, and Nonso and Aisha nodded in agreement. I didn't buy this but I felt better because it was one thing I couldn't share with my mom and now it was out in the open. Nonso was already learning to drive, the first among us to do so. She almost crashed her mother's car because she asked her mom about a conversation she'd partially overheard between her mom and aunt and discovered that they were discussing her grandmother's first marriage, to a rich woman. Aisha was the boldest of us, boywise, and she shared with us the details of her first kiss with a boy three years older—a seventeen-year-old in his second year of university.

———

When Nonso and Aisha came to persuade us to join the protest in front of Mrs. Haastrup's house, Solape and I were in the classroom area studying with Wunmi, the class teacher's pet. Solape was my only rival for first place in math and we were studying together for a test the next day. We were the lone protest holdouts from the fourth form.

"This is big, more important than your study routine," Aisha insisted, looking at me because she knew Solape would be a harder sell.

Solape was a month older than Aisha, even though she was almost a foot shorter, the oldest but shortest of the four of us. When Aisha tried to be bossy, as she sometimes did, Solape would say softly but firmly, "Aburo, I'm older than you. You need to listen to the wisdom of your elders. I don't have to listen to you." This always cracked Nonso and me up because Aisha never had a good comeback to that.

The new principal had dismissed two of our favorite teachers, for physics and biology, because they refused to suck up to her.

"We've gone two months without a physics teacher," Aisha said.

"It's not like you can write 'we never got a chance to cover this' when the SSS exams come around," Nonso said.

Solape just shook her head. "She'll eventually hire new teachers. We have almost two years before those exams."

Aisha rolled her eyes. "So you have no problem with the fact that she fired teachers in the middle of the term before getting replacements? Who is she punishing, the teachers or us?"

"My father didn't send me to school to protest." This was Wunmi's sole contribution to the discussion.

"I see," Aisha said. "You're on the science track, aren't you? He's fine with reducing your chances of going to university because you never got taught biology or physics? And he sent you to school to learn to let everyone walk all over you, abi?" Aisha's face twitched as she spoke.

Wunmi laid her head on her desk and shut her eyes by way of response, and Solape put a comforting hand on her back, looking angrily at Aisha. "Stop talking nonsense, please.

There's no need for that," Solape said. There was no argument Aisha could make at this point to convince her; Solape liked Wunmi, Aisha did not, and putting Wunmi down as she had was the best way to get Solape on Wunmi's side.

Aisha pushed on anyway. "Okay, maybe none of you is planning to be a doctor, so you don't care about losing the physics and biology teachers, but what about the food? We barely get enough now and forget about decent meat. She's chopping money. Remi, surely you can't ignore that!"

The food portions in the dining hall had shrunk since Mrs. Haastrup had taken up the principal's job, but everyone knew she was getting the same amount from the government as the previous principal. Meals that once left us sated now had to be followed by large quantities of water so we felt full. I sometimes woke up in the night, belly rumbling. Mrs. Haastrup was especially cunning—on visiting days when our parents were around, the dining hall portions magically doubled, and we received choice cuts of beef in place of skin, tripe, gristle, and liver.

I nodded. I actually agreed with all the reasons for the protest and wasn't afraid of confronting the principal. I just didn't think that standing in front of Mrs. Haastrup's house screaming would bring about the changes we wanted. I wasn't sure what would, though; the woman seemed impervious to reason.

"Okay, I'm coming with you," I said.

"Remi, you're such a longathroat," Nonso teased as we joined the group of fourth and fifth formers heading to the principal's house.

"Such a shame that only the mention of food got to you." Aisha shook her head in mock sorrow.

I grinned, refusing to be baited. "Of course. I can get a biology or physics tutor at home. The absence of good food will kill me now!"

———

A car went by the administrative area. We heard the engine rev, as the driver took in the scene of girls throwing and smashing things and floored it. It was full dark now, so I couldn't tell whose car it was but we started to laugh.

After smashing all the glass in the administrative office area, we walked up the mound toward the classrooms, armed with stones and tree branches, fully intending to do more of the same. I saw lights, full beams bearing down on us, and then the driver cut them out. The car passed one of the streetlamps lining the road from the main gate and I noticed it was a navy-blue Peugeot pickup. The kind driven by the police.

"Olopa," I screamed, dropping the stones I was carrying and heading back in the direction we'd come from, to the farm area where we planted corn and yams for our agriculture class. Nonso and Aisha followed me. The principal was the only person with a working phone in her residence. It had never occurred to us that she might call the police. Girls scattered in every direction and we hoped it was just the one van. We hid behind some plants in the farm, lying flat on the ground between raised mounds of earth. I tried to steady my ragged breath but couldn't—at any moment, the gleam of a flashlight could expose us. I wondered whether there were any snakes near us and shuddered, my skin crawling with reptile-loathing. The farm was eerily quiet. The silence around us was eventually broken by the drunken chirping of lovelorn crickets and a rustling that I convinced myself was leaves fluttering in the breeze.

After what seemed like hours, Nonso said, "Remi, Aisha, I don't think they're coming for us."

We dusted ourselves off and headed back toward the classrooms. The dorms would still be locked; there was no point heading that way. If questioned, we'd decided to say that we were with the group in the dining area and had just finished our jollof rice. We got to the fourth-form classroom block just in time to see Solape and Wunmi being pushed toward the pickup with their hands behind their backs. Solape looked frightened and even smaller than usual.

Aisha shouted, "Where are you taking them?"

The policemen ignored her.

"I started this. Those two didn't join in, they were studying. Arrest me instead." Aisha grabbed one of the policemen by the arm. He turned roughly toward her and then shrank back in recognition. "Omo minister ma ni yen!"

When Aisha's father was made minister of defense, the newspapers ran a spread featuring him and his family: Aisha's mother in a flowing purple Senegalese boubou and floppy almost-afro, Aisha grinning, same complexion as her mother but her hair done up in cornrows, and her brother, who was dark with bulbous eyes, just like his dad. Aisha said it was her mom's Cherokee ancestry that left her hair unable to stand up straight. Neither Solape nor Nonso nor I knew what that meant, but we certainly didn't have that problem. We did know that Aisha's parents had met in the U.S., and we laughed at Aisha for switching accents when she talked to her mom on visiting day. She'd brought a few of the newspapers with photo spreads for Aisha to see, and Aisha had shared them with us. Apparently the policemen also read those newspapers. There was nothing Aisha could do that would make them arrest her. They bundled Wunmi and Solape into the van and drove off.

———

Wunmi returned to school the next afternoon. She was trembling and her eyes were red and sunken into her head. Our teachers had refused to teach until the two girls arrested were returned to school, so we'd spent the morning sitting in our classrooms swapping rumors about what had happened to Wunmi and Solape. They took them to Kirikiri Maximum Security Prison just to scare them, one girl said. They only take armed robbers and murderers there, said another, skeptically.

When Wunmi appeared in our classroom, we cheered. She was immediately surrounded.

"Where'd they take you?"

"To the police station. They put us in a cell next to thieves."

"Oti o." We were shocked at that.

"Where's Solape?" I asked.

"She's in the hospital. She had an asthma attack, and of course they didn't let her take her inhaler when they took us from here. At first, they thought she was pretending even though I was begging them for help and saying she had asthma and couldn't breathe properly."

My blood ran cold at that; I tried to imagine Solape without her inhaler in the middle of an asthma attack. I looked around the classroom and saw Solape's inhaler still sitting on top of her desk. No one had touched it. I began to cry. Nonso and Aisha came over to comfort me.

"She'll be okay," said Aisha. "The hospital will know what to do."

"If only she'd joined us," said Nonso. "She would actually have been safer with us."

"Oh, shut up," I said, filled with a sudden dislike for both her and Aisha and glaring at both of them. "You don't know that. I should have stayed with her in the classroom. I should have stayed."

I'd never spoken to either of them with such hostility. Nonso looked stunned and sort of crumpled into herself. Aisha looked at me and opened her mouth to say something. A strangled squeak came out and then she started to cry as well. Aisha never cried. I gathered myself together, hugged her, and grabbed Nonso's hand. "I'm sorry. It's okay. You're right. The hospital will know what to do. They probably have extra inhalers that she can use."

Back at the dorms that night, Aisha, Nonso, and I sat in front of Queen Amina House after lights-out, and for the first time ever, prayed together. We prayed for Solape's safe return and prayed that God would bless the doctors and nurses taking care of her. I felt much better after that, like we had done something useful to bring her back to us.

———

The second morning after the riot, our math teacher walked in front of the class, staring at her feet. She coughed and swayed and then raised her head to look directly at the girls. There was a strange sheen to her eyes and her face looked puffy and swollen. Solape, she said, had fallen unconscious on the way to the hospital. The doctors had tried everything they could but she just never woke up.

Girls gasped as she spoke. Everyone looked confused, waiting for the teacher to announce that this was some kind of cruel hoax, expecting her to take back her words. She didn't.

A girl at the front said, "Does that mean she is in a coma?"

I held my breath, praying that this was what the teacher meant—they couldn't wake her up but she would wake up by herself when she was ready.

"That's not what I'm saying." Tears started to slide down the teacher's face and she wiped them away quickly.

After almost half a minute of staring at the math teacher, I said, "No, Miss Adelugba. No. That can't be true. Asthma doesn't kill people." I suddenly felt cold, then lightheaded. I could feel my heart beat faster as a slow flush of heat swept from my chest up my neck to my face. The air pressed down on me, thick and heavy. I knew that I had to get to the front of the class and shut her dishonest mouth. Solape would be back with us soon. I knew it. We'd prayed about it. I moved toward the teacher and Nonso ran forward, hugged me, and held on tight. Her body was shaking uncontrollably. I said, "Nonso, they're lying. They're lying to us. Where is she?" Nonso held on and I couldn't move. She didn't utter a sound. The teacher looked stricken but she didn't say anything more.

Aisha was sobbing now. "She didn't join in. She never joined us. Why did they take her?"

It was a question that didn't need an answer. We all knew why. Solape and Wunmi were the only students within easy reach of the policemen when they arrived. And it wasn't immediately obvious that their parents were rich or powerful or anything else that might stay a policeman's hand. It was just easier to assume they were pretending to study and had been a part of the riot than to take them at their word.

————

Three days after Solape died, our entire school was suspended for a month under orders from the Ministry of Education. When we got back, we had another principal, Mrs. Rotimi, a tall, stern-looking woman who had been the first female principal of a boys' boarding school. We had the troublemaker tag now. We also had replacement biology and physics teachers. None of us cared. Aisha looked depressed, her head on her desk every time I turned around. I don't know why, but that annoyed me. I wanted Solape back, wanted Solape as I remembered her in math class, the one class in which she seemed upbeat, hand raised, face glowing as she prepared to answer a question, a confident smile softening her features, hinting at the beautiful woman she would never become.

REFLECTIONS FROM THE HOOD OF A CAR

1991

SEGUN

I've never met a policeman I liked on any continent. My first brush with the species was in Ibadan, at the age of eight. That encounter started, as this one does, with my mother's car. Then, it was a battered white Peugeot 504 with no air conditioner. My younger sister and I sat in the back as my mom nosed the car through the Dugbe market traffic. The chatter from hawkers and their bargain-minded customers swirled around us, mingling with the blat of car horns, discordant and unceasing.

We'd gone to the market to buy black cloth. My mom's tailor was going to make us winter coats—a short jacket for me and long coats for my mother and sister—because we were leaving in a few months to join my father in the U.S. My sister and I were excited about moving to the U.S., but if my mother was, she didn't show it. Unlike my dad, she'd never traveled outside Nigeria. He'd told me many stories about his time in England (for school) and America (for more school) and Brazil (out of curiosity). Brazil because his maternal great-grandfather, whom he'd actually met when he was a young boy, was a Da Silva. António Da Silva to be precise; a gifted carpenter born somewhere in the western part of Nigeria (he didn't remember exactly where), captured and shipped to Bahia when he was no more than ten years old. António knew that he was Yoruba, still spoke the language, and left Brazil for Lagos in 1890, a few years after he earned his freedom. Brazil was the only place outside Nigeria that I'd heard my mother express any interest in visiting, and I think it was because she was convinced my father had made up the stories he told us about eating the best akara he'd ever tasted in Bahia.

It had taken a long time to find fabric thick enough to please my mother. In shop after shop, sellers brought out black cotton poplin cloth that could be worn without collapsing in the Ibadan heat, but my mother simply shook her head. "It's too thin," she would say, patiently. "I told you we need it for the cold." The women stared at her baffled. How cold could it possibly get in this place she claimed to be going to? Some argued with her about the superior quality of their goods, others simply got annoyed at her pickiness. Finally, one told her go to Iya Momodu's. "She sells cloth for away," the woman said, washing her hands of us. Iya Momodu had thick black wool cloth that made my mother exclaim in delight and clap her hands, after the frustration of visiting eight stores with no luck. Of course, her elation was noted by Iya Momodu and meant that a long and healthy back-and-forth on the price ensued, my mother slowly bringing the cost per yard down until they agreed on a number.

Sitting in the back of the car after the purchase, I was tired of the haggling and the midday swelter and just wanted to get home. I remember willing my mother to drive faster, willing the warm breeze drifting through the rolled-down windows to pick up, provide some relief. Wishful thinking. Sweat dripped down my forehead as I fought to keep my eyes open in the heat.

After a half hour of inching jerkily forward, all traffic stopped, which was not unusual. My mom turned to ask my sister how she was doing, since she sometimes got carsick. I don't remember my sister's answer, but I can't forget the blur of the policeman's horsewhip as it came down on my mother's neck through the open window. I'd never heard that sound before, the high-pitched fusion of agony and panic that came from her throat. I never have since. It drilled into my bones, tightened every muscle in my body, pooled hot liquid behind my eyelids.

The officer moved on casually to the vehicle behind us, flicking the koboko as he walked, leaving my mother gasping, fighting to hold the tears in.

"The governor is coming" is what I recall the policeman saying after the whip hit. And I thought, *What does that have to do with whipping my mother?*

I can still feel the rush of blood to my temples, a burning need to do *something* to rid my memory of her strangled cry. When I opened the door of the car and ran after the policeman, I had no clear plan. Just got close to him, dropped to my knees, fixed my teeth on his leg, and held on. I have never been so happy to hear another human being howl. The policeman grabbed my head and pulled so hard that I felt pain in all the tendons in my neck, then threw me. I fell backward, legs twisted under thighs. Now realizing that I could be in danger, I struggled to drag myself away from him and toward the safety of my mother's car, elbows scraping the hot tarmac in my haste. I wasn't sure what else he might do, but I couldn't get my limbs untangled. Next thing I knew, my mother was by my side, pulling me away, cowering before the officer. She shielded my body with hers, started to plead with him on my behalf. "Sorry, sir. Na small boy. Na small boy. Sorry, sir."

He was too stunned and in too much pain to say much initially. When he finally collected himself, he said, "*Boy*, I would have given you the beating of your life, if your mother hadn't come to save you."

I looked him right in the eyes as he spoke, something I'd never done with an adult outside my family. Fear forgotten, my anger came rushing back. I was ready to take the beating if he still wanted to give it. He looked away first, mumbled something under his breath about *children of nowadays*, and walked on.

"Segun, why did you do that?" My mother placed a hand on the back of my neck and pushed me toward the Peugeot. "Do you know what he could have done to you?" Her voice was unsteady. A fan-shaped series of welts had sprouted on the left side of her neck; they seemed to mirror the elaborate corn-rows crisscrossing her scalp. Once we were back in the safety of the car, she kept swiveling her head from side to side. My sister dug her fingers into my arm, and her small body, shuddering with sobs, made my own shake. I wiped the tears from her face.

I said, "He whipped you . . . I had to do something."

The sense of satisfaction I felt started to wane. Biting an adult was an offense my mother was likely to punish. Severely. My arms started to tremble, so I wrapped them around my sister and hugged her sideways, waiting to hear what my punishment would be. Silence. I tilted my head up slightly, opening my mouth to squeak out something more, something that might lessen the punishment. I wasn't prepared for the smile on my mother's face as she studied mine, still not saying a word. She never mentioned the policeman again.

———

Now, here I am, ten years later, in the Bronx. I'm eighteen and splayed out facedown next to my cousin Debo on the hood of my mother's dark blue Honda Accord. It's Debo's first trip to New York; he returns to Nigeria in three weeks. We lie beneath the number 4 train's elevated tracks, mannequins in the Bronx summer heat, while officers Murphy and DiSorbo try to determine what, if anything, we can be accused of. DiSorbo reminds me of that Ibadan officer: tall, cocky, with a wide jaw and flared nostrils, a tic in his face that makes me think he is short-tempered. Murphy is a rookie, I can tell. He is a squat, hairy man who doesn't fully inhabit his blue uniform. I ignore DiSorbo, decide to speak to Murphy. His eyes dart to my face and then slide away, almost apologetically. He won't look at me directly when I ask, politely, why we're being hassled. Requests quietly that we lie facedown against the hood of the car. There is no threat, no malice, no energy in his voice. I wonder whether it's his first day on the job.

———

Ten years in the U.S. have stretched my frame out to its full six-foot-five-inch length, though I'm still a bit on the lean side. Those years haven't dulled a craving for the food I grew up eating. After my dad left Nigeria for the U.S., I spent countless Ibadan nights dreaming of New York: the skyscrapers, cars whizzing past unrestricted by traffic jams, pedestrians streaming down sidewalks and streets without fear. My dreams never featured food. When we finally joined him, I realized too late how deficient those dreams were. I've gradually learned to tolerate pizza but don't have much use for salads. I can inhale a bacon Whopper with cheese in twelve seconds. Still, nothing beats pounded yam in my ranking of favorite foods. Pounded yam is the reason that Debo and I have made the trip to the Bronx from Yonkers.

It's my first summer break from the United World College I attend in New Mexico. Since I can't afford to travel anyplace else, I'm visiting my mom and sister in Yonkers. After my dad died of cancer three years ago, I learned how to make okra soup and how to mash the pounded yam smooth in my mom's cake mixer until it looked like the real thing. My sister had just turned thirteen when Dad died. I was fifteen. She and I figured our mom had enough to deal with. When Mom got a second job at an old people's home to help pay our private school fees, we took over all the cooking and housecleaning.

Some of her charges are too far gone from dementia to remember who they are. They birthed children who have long since left the difficult task of changing their aging parents' diapers to people like my mom. The lucid ones share stories that my mom retells when she gets home.

"It's a shame when you know so much, but nobody will listen," she says.

My sister and I used to pay attention to the stories when she first started the job. Then they started blurring, running into one another until we didn't remember who fled communism in Hungary, whose son was a gifted flautist, and whose daughter hadn't visited in ten years out of sheer spite. More important, we stopped caring. We didn't tell my mom this, though. Her eyes went soft and unfocused when she talked about them—it was almost like sharing their stories with us was her way of making sure that we would never forget hers.

———

Debo's father came to visit us a year after my dad died. We'd moved from the airy three-bedroom apartment we had when Dad was alive to a dark, cramped basement-level one-bedroom with a pullout couch in the living room. I slept on the floor, Baba Debo took my place on the pullout couch, and my mom and sister shared the bedroom as usual. Within a week, he asked us to move back to Nigeria.

"This is not living," he said, patting his potbelly. "You spend almost all your time working and for what?" His neck wattles shook as he spoke.

My mother shrugged. "We like it here. There's nothing wrong with hard work. I'm proud to do it." She gestured at my sister and me. "They're happy to do it."

I got up from the dining chair where I was sitting and stood next to my mom, placing my hand lightly on her shoulder to show Baba Debo that I was in full support of whatever she said. My sister followed my lead and stood on my mother's right side.

He smiled. "I see my brother's stubbornness was contagious."

With the help of his army friends, my uncle had made enough money siphoning oil from pipelines to buy a private jet. My father had been deeply ashamed of his younger brother. *I don't make my money like a common thief*, he'd said to me when I asked why we couldn't go to London every few months like Baba Debo's family. *Remember, your good name is the only thing that matters.* I was six at the time, and more interested in visiting Madame Tussauds than saving my good name, but somehow, I knew not to share this.

———

Today, my mom has time off work and she insisted on making my favorite meal. We had no yam tubers at home, so Debo and I went to a West African grocery store in the Bronx to buy them. We cruised down the Major Deegan, Public Enemy pumping from the speakers, took the exit that follows the elevated train tracks, parked in front of a window advertising Bournvita and Mary's Boflot. In the small, airless shop, the dizzying smell of stockfish mixed with fermented locust beans had Debo pinching his nostrils together. I jabbed my elbow into his ribs and he dropped his hand quickly.

"Good afternoon, Ma," I said to the woman who owned the store. She smiled through a bulletproof glass partition.

"Segun. How are you? You've grown taller! Your mom is always talking about how well you're doing in school. But why did you go so far away?"

"They gave me a full scholarship," I said.

She nodded. "Ooooh. Yes, that helps. That helps a lot. Please greet your mother for me."

"I will."

I paid for three hefty yam tubers and we quickly made our way to the street. Murphy and DiSorbo were waiting near my mom's car as we approached it. DiSorbo said, *Is this your car? We want to talk to you*, and Debo dropped the shopping bag full of yams.

———

So why are Debo and I now splayed out on the hood? I suspect it's the newness of my mother's leased car, which recently replaced a thirdhand Volvo that stalled on the highway. The Volvo decided to stay dead even though there was no money for a new car. Reliable transportation is the key to keeping her current jobs. I could try explaining all that to DiSorbo, but I don't think I can find the precise set of words that will get through to him. Every time I open my mouth, I feel DiSorbo is disappointed, that he wants me to speak a language he's more familiar with. A language I have refused to learn, though many men in blue have tried to teach it to me, through stops for driving, for sitting, for walking, for shopping, for "loitering" while waiting to take my sister home from her friend's place, for always being the wrong person in the right place at the right time.

My dad used to say, "Segun, Nigeria is hard on the body. America is hard on the mind. You have to be mentally tough here. Tutu like ice. Don't lose your temper. Promise me." He started to tell me this when I hit six feet at the age of twelve and the old white ladies in the apartment building we lived in at the time began to clutch their handbags when I got in the elevator, the same way they'd always clutched their handbags when he got in. My mother would get upset when he talked like that; she didn't understand why he would bring us halfway around the world to be "so negative just because of a few stupid people." I wish he could see me now, see how calm I can be.

DiSorbo speaks of searching without a warrant, and I tamp down the rage that came on so easily when I was eight, push it down deep—this asshole here will not see me lose it. I turn my head toward Murphy, knowing as I do so that it's a waste of time. He looks away. Suddenly, I'm filled with a contempt for Murphy that blunts my anger toward DiSorbo. DiSorbo at least wears his thuggishness and arrogance openly. Murphy will probably spend a good part of his life following along and saying nothing while his guilty eyes plead for understanding.

"Go ahead," I say. "Knock yourself out."

Debo is shaking slightly as he lies beside me on the hood. He's just fifteen, didn't expect this adventure, isn't sure what to do with himself.

"Lie very still," I whisper. "Whatever they do, no sudden moves."

"Okay. But what did we do?"

"I'll explain later," I say. "I think they're running the plates on the car to make sure it isn't stolen. The tall cop is on a power trip but I can tell the shorter one doesn't want to hassle us, so we won't be here too long."

He doesn't seem reassured by my response. I try to think of a way to cheer him up. I caught him earlier today staring at a picture of my girlfriend, Remi, that I left on the dining room table. He had a hungry look that made me happy inside.

I whisper to Debo, "You were asking me how I got together with Remi."

Debo nods, the worry on his face now replaced by an expectant, eager look. He's not bad-looking, but it seems he hasn't had much luck with the girls at the British boarding school he attends in Togo.

I knew Remi would be mine three weeks after we met at the United World College. She asked me to walk with her to get a new radio because she wasn't yet comfortable with American accents. "What if they give me the wrong change and I need to argue with them?"

I thought this was kind of silly, but didn't tell Remi. The salesclerk at the store had angry red acne pits covering every inch of her face.

I said, "A fe ra gbohun-gbohun."

"'Scuse me?" The salesclerk dug her fingers into a freshly healed scab on her jawline and began to worry it free.

"Mo ni a fe ra gbohun-gbohun, abi eti e di ni?" I kept a straight face as I repeated the request for a radio and asked whether she was deaf or something.

Remi clapped her hand over her mouth to keep from screeching out loud. The salesclerk went to get the store manager to help sort out the language problem.

The man waddled over, wet patches spreading under his arms and down his chest, his immense gut preceding the rest of him. "How may I help you?" He spoke as loudly as he could, drawing each word out slowly and waving his fingers in the air in some sort of sign language designed to boost our comprehension.

"I asked her where I could find a radio is all," I said in my best New York accent.

The clerk gasped as the manager cut his eyes at her, annoyed, and led us to the right section of the store.

Remi giggled once the man moved on. "You are so crazy, you better watch out."

"Yeah, crazy like a fox," I said, and kissed her on the lips right there in the aisle. She kissed me back before she pushed me away.

I whisper the story to Debo. He starts to laugh, a high-pitched snicker punctuated with snorts that makes me lose it. Murphy and DiSorbo come around.

"What's so funny?" DiSorbo asks, squinting his eyes.

"The fact that you're an ass." I say it in a low mumble.

Debo almost chokes.

"Whatchu say?"

My dad's voice is in my head going Segun! Segun, I told you, tutu like ice. You have got to be careful. My heart starts to beat faster. Dad, I don't think he heard me.

"We're running late for Mass." I twist my head a little and give DiSorbo my best approximation of an angelic smile. "Being devout Catholics and all."

DiSorbo places the flat of his palm on the side of my head, mashing my face into the hood of the car as Debo looks on in horror. I start to ball up my fists and then I stop, let my whole body go slack. He's not expecting that. He eases the pressure on my head and says we can go.

———

We travel in silence under the train tracks, then leave them behind at the Van Cortlandt Park stop as we head back to the Major Deegan. When we pass the sign welcoming us to Yonkers, Debo says in a deep voice, "What's so funny?"

I say, loudly this time, "The fact that you're an ass."

He starts laughing, hard, just as a wave of nausea hits me. I pull over to the side of the road and race for the grassy verge, leaving the key in the ignition. My body spasms and it feels like everything inside me is fighting to come up. I'm shaking, undone, my very being violently rejecting the scene we left behind. My silence. My acceptance. My shame. Swallowed, buried deep because what I really want—oh, what I want is to wrap my hands gently around DiSorbo's neck, tilt his head back just enough that he can *see* me. Really see me. No *tutu like ice*, my raw feelings, just the two of us, that arrogant smirk off his face, replaced with a dash of fear and definitely, respect. An understanding of who I am, my place in this world as well as his. But the guns make that impossible, bullets and fear equal death every time because my face will never evoke his son, his brother, his father, his uncles, his teenaged self, carefree, living on the edge before the rigors of the police academy made their mark. Debo kneels down beside me and I look sideways at him. His eyes are wide, mouth a frightened O, and then he asks me whether I'm doing okay.

"Tremendous, champ," I say in a faux British accent, once the dry heaving stops. "Never better."

He looks like he's about to burst into tears but he's determined to help out.

"I could drive us home," he says.

"And really give them a reason to pull us over." I sit back

on the grass away from the puke, put my head between my legs, and breathe.

"No, no. You've taught me well." He lays on the flattery thick.

I've been teaching him how to drive on a dead-end road not far from our apartment, but he's fifteen, unlicensed, and not yet ready for the highway.

"I'll be okay soon," I say. "We're just five miles from home."

He looks relieved and it's only then that I realize he wasn't actually keen on driving. I stand up, squeeze his shoulder, and smile. He looks up at me and smiles back. I head back to the driver's seat and wait for him to put on his seat belt.

Did that ever happen to you? I ask my dad. He doesn't whisper back the way he sometimes does in my head. I'm on my own now. Easing the car back onto the highway, I grip the steering wheel tight, focus on a blue patch on the horizon interrupted by deep red splotches from the setting sun. I suppress an urge to scream because once I start, I'm not sure I'll ever stop. And I have definitely lost my appetite for pounded yam.

GUARDIAN ANGEL OF ELMINA

1983

NONSO

Lagos gives me a stomachache. It happens every time we visit from Ibadan; my stomach knots up and I have to press on it with both hands to make the pain stop because there are just people, people everywhere. Too many people. I like Ibadan, I was born there, but my mom was born in Lagos, so her eyes get big and shiny when we visit and she says, "Nonso, look, look," as she points at buildings and tries to tell me how it was when she was a child. Basically, it has changed and it changes some more every time we visit. I much prefer Ibadan, the UI campus where we live on Sankore Avenue. From Sankore Avenue, I can walk to Kurunmi Road to play with my friends or I can walk to Awba Dam and sit by myself, looking at the waters of the lake. We're not allowed to swim in Awba Dam, but I love how beautiful and peaceful it is there. I can walk to the main gate by myself, when my mom lets me go buy some of my boarding school provisions from Agbowo. My mom says UI is not the real Ibadan, but I don't agree. Don't get me wrong, I like Bodija too and Ashi Village and Agodi, but UI is my favorite place on earth.

Anyway, we are heading to my uncle Uchenna's house in Ikoyi. Uncle Uchenna is my mom's oldest brother and he and his wife are very rich. My mom is the last born of her family, just like I am; Uncle Uchenna is fifteen years older than she is. She takes me to visit him at least once a year, just the two of us, but I don't like going; he's so serious about everything and his children are much older than me and don't live at home anymore, so there's no one for me to play with. He doesn't like the fact that my mom and I switch from speaking Igbo to speaking Yoruba to each other several times in the same conversation (mostly because my Yoruba is slightly better than my Igbo, so I'm more comfortable speaking it). He calls my mother by her full Igbo name, Nwabundo. Everyone else, even my grandmother calls her Wura, the name given to her by her Yoruba godmother, their neighbor when my mom was born. Wura means "gold," so I love that name, but Uncle Uchenna won't even say it.

"Nwabundo," he always says, "you can't trust people who say wa when they want you to move closer to them."

Wa in my language means "run away, run, run, run as fast as your legs can carry you from danger." In Yoruba, it means "come here." My mom laughs every time he says this, an exasperated laugh accompanied by head-shaking, and then changes the subject. He's lived in Lagos most of his life and speaks both Igbo and Yoruba fluently. His wife is half-Yoruba; her mother is from Lagos and her father is from Anioma, just like us. She doesn't even react when he says these things.

When I ask my mother why he says that, she shakes her head and says, "Nonso, the war was very difficult. Many things happened but, thank God, we are all here."

My mother once told me that some of Uncle Uchenna's Yoruba in-laws hid him and saved his life during the war, but other people did bad things to him. My mother and father were far away in America for graduate school during the Biafran War. Sometimes I think she feels guilty that they weren't home with their families.

———

We'll visit Uncle Uchenna for two days and then he'll drive us to Ghana to celebrate my eleventh birthday, which already happened when I was away at school. It's not what I asked for, but my mom is different—all my friends agree that my mom is different. My friends Aisha and Remi have been to London but my friend Solape and I have not. I wanted to go back to boarding school this autumn and let Solape know that she's the only one who hasn't been to London, but when I told my mom what I wanted for my eleventh birthday, she said no. Just like that, no. I told her that Aisha and Remi have been and Solape and I haven't, but she didn't care.

"Nwam, you will first see Africa before you see London," she said.

"But Mummy, we've been to Kenya and Zimbabwe and Botswana!"

"And then? Is that all of Africa?"

"So I'm never going to London, then?"

"Nonso, come here, I didn't say that." Her face softened, and she pulled me to her and gave me a hug. "Don't look so sad. Maybe when you're sixteen."

"But that's years and years and years from now!" My mom gets so unreasonable sometimes.

———

My mom had my three brothers first, then me. She's a history professor and, because I'm the last born and my brothers are all in university, she takes me with her to conferences, sometimes with our house help, Nkechi, to keep me company.

When we visited east and southern Africa, it was 1981 and I was nine years old. We went to Nairobi in Kenya, Bulawayo and Harare in Zimbabwe, and Gaborone in Botswana. My mom studies the Kingdom of Zimbabwe, which is different from the country of Zimbabwe because it existed a long, long time ago. Like how the Kingdom of Ghana is different from Ghana and the Kingdom of Mali is different from Mali. My history teacher at Fiditi, Mr. Kolawole, taught us about Ibn Battuta, who was from Morocco. He says Ibn Battuta traveled to Mali in the 1300s by camel and met Mansa Musa, the king of Mali. Mansa Musa went from Timbuktu to Mecca for hajj and gave away so much gold that the price went down across the whole world. I tried to imagine that much gold. Gold everywhere. Mr. Kolawole likes to talk about salt and gold a lot. He was one of my mom's students at UI, and he's always strict with me and stops by to give my mom a report about how I'm doing in class when she comes to Fiditi to see me on visiting day. He's an alakoba, always trying to get me in trouble, so I avoid him as much as possible, but I still like history class.

———

For my first trip outside Nigeria, when I was nine, my mom and I took a Kenya Airways flight to Jomo Kenyatta Airport in Nairobi. Nairobi sounded to me like a city with lots of naira, a city where naira is their obi, their heart and soul. I knew they must be very rich.

I told my mom this and she shook her head. "Nonso, how do you come up with this silly stuff? The name Nairobi has nothing to do with naira and anyway, they use shillings in Kenya, not naira."

I retreated to my book, really annoyed and determined to

ignore her. I thought then that maybe I should have stayed at home with my dad; at least he'd take me to his physics lab and I could bother all the graduate students. He doesn't make me feel stupid the way my mom does sometimes.

We spent two days in Nairobi, then we were off to Botswana. There was no direct flight from Kenya to Botswana; we had to fly to South Africa to catch another plane. We flew over an area with lots of blue and green—many, many swimming pools and nice lawns. Then we saw hundreds of brown and gray shacks, one after the other.

My mom said, "This is Johannesburg." She looked very upset.

Our flight from Kenya was delayed, so by the time we landed at Jan Smuts Airport in Johannesburg, we'd missed the flight to Botswana for the day. My mom paced up and down, I'd never seen her so agitated. "I can't believe this," she said. "Nigeria has no diplomatic relations with South Africa because of apartheid, so we can't leave the airport. We'll have to spend the night here at Jan Smuts." She spat the name out like it was something dirty and flared her nostrils.

I didn't see what was so bad about spending a night at the airport and I was happy running around the terminal until I convinced myself that a uniformed guard with a machine gun was following me. I ran into the bathroom. When I emerged, I saw his scowling face, so I quickly found my mom and stayed glued to her side.

"They have a hotel here," she said. "We won't have to lie down on the floor of the terminal."

I was enjoying our adventure, now that the armed man no longer seemed interested in me, and I didn't much care whether we slept on the terminal floor or in a hotel room. I had a lot to tell my friends in Ibadan already. A gray-faced woman with short hair that stood up took us to our quarters, a small room with a narrow bed and one window that looked out onto large gray concrete planters that sat empty and made me think of coffins.

"This place is so ugly," I said to my mom.

She was fuming about something, I didn't understand what, so I tried to cheer her up. Maybe a good meal would do the trick.

"I'm hungry," I said. "Do you think they have amala with okra soup at any of the restaurants here?"

She stared at me and started to laugh, "Ke ke ke ke ke." When she could breathe again, she said, "Nonso, I'd love to see that starch-faced toad of a woman eat amala and okra. That would be something."

We headed back toward the bustle of the terminal and sat at a restaurant. I noticed that all the servers were black, unlike the armed guard and the gray-faced woman. They seemed awed by my mother.

"How old is your son?" our waiter asked my mother, smiling widely at me.

At nine, I had very short hair, no breasts, and I was wearing a T-shirt and jeans, but couldn't he see my face? Everyone except my mom said I looked prettier when I cut my hair short. She'd wanted me to keep it long, but I thought I would have trouble finding someone to braid it for me in boarding school.

"I'm not a boy, I'm a girl," I said, very curtly.

"Oh. I'm sorry, miss," he said, his eyes glinting in a way that told me he wasn't sorry at all. "I saw your hair and I thought . . . My mistake." I could see he was trying not to laugh.

I didn't see eba or amala or yam or anything remotely resembling real food on the restaurant menu.

"Mummy, there's nothing for me to eat," I said.

"You can't expect every country you visit to have Nigerian food," she replied. "Anyway, this menu is entirely British food."

I scrunched up my nose and sulked until, finally, my mom ordered something for me. That was my first time eating steak-and-kidney pie. I hope that it is my last.

We flew from South Africa to Botswana and spent a few days at a Holiday Inn in Gaborone with a gigantic swimming pool and people selling beautiful crocheted hats and dresses near the entrance. I asked my mom to buy me a crocheted dress, but she laughed and shook her head no. I passed the time splashing in the shallow end of the pool, taking breaks to eat butter beans and toasted cheese sandwiches and staring at people. Soon, it was time for us to catch a train. My mother said it would take us from Gaborone to Francistown, near the border with Zimbabwe. We caught a taxi to the train station and I pressed my nose to the car window, gaping at everything we passed. It took us ten hours to get to Francistown from Gaborone. I loved the rhythm of the train, the way it went shuga-shuga-shuga-shuga. I stared out of the window at the buildings and people and houses and shrubs and trees flying by until it got too dark and I lay back on the narrow bed in the sleeper car and dozed off. I'd never been on a train before. In Francistown, we caught a bus to Bulawayo and my mom started to tell me how it was 1981 in Zimbabwe and something about liberation, but I was too busy observing different people on the bus (taking care to look away before she said I was being rude) and staring out the bus window to really listen. We met up with a friend of hers from school in America and the woman had a daughter my age, so we played checkers and hopscotch and I taught her ten-ten, Nigerian style. We talked and talked and talked and I told her all about how I was looking forward to going to boarding school once the summer holidays were over, and instead of being jealous, she said she would never want to go to boarding school and anyway, her parents wouldn't allow it. I couldn't understand it. Why wouldn't she want to go to boarding school?

When we got back to Ibadan, I said, "Mummy, Zimbabwe was my favorite part of the whole trip!"

Her eyes sparkled and she smiled. Then she asked me why.

"Because they have Fanta grape! We only have Fanta orange in Nigeria; I've never had Fanta grape before."

———

During our trip to Ghana, my mom was going to attend a history conference. We were going to stay with another friend of hers from graduate school, Aunty Nana-Yaa, who taught at the University of Ghana, Legon. Uncle Uchenna would drive us there, spend a few days doing business in Accra, and head back to Lagos; then, after two weeks, we would fly back to Ibadan on Ghana Airways. Uncle Uchenna drove us first to Cotonou and Aflao before we got to Accra. There were lots and lots of fishing boats in Aflao and we saw fishermen haul in nets of writhing fish. Just nets and flashes of silver everywhere and I ran up and down the beach watching them, breathing in the smells of fish and salt water and smoke; it was wonderful. I'd like to go to Aflao again.

———

After my mom's conference in Accra, Aunty Nana-Yaa drove us to Elmina Castle. We woke up early and left Accra at six in the morning. It took us about three hours to get to Elmina. When we arrived, I saw a massive whitewashed building near the Atlantic Ocean. We went on a tour and started out in an area with a chapel. Listening to our tour guide, I realized that the castle wasn't a castle for princes and princesses but an old fort built by the Portuguese and then captured by the Dutch, a place where people were kept before they were taken from Africa and turned into slaves. They were people that looked like me. Some my age, some older, some younger. I looked at my mom, but she didn't look back at me and we kept following the tour guide, but I wanted to go home. I really wanted to go home. We left the large airy spaces upstairs and went down some steps to where it was dark and gloomy and the air felt heavy somehow; I had to push myself to move through it. The tour guide said something about dungeons and slaves. I started to feel really cold. I folded my arms across my chest to try to keep warm. We went into a dark room. The tour guide said it used to hold more than one hundred women, but it was so small, I couldn't imagine how they would all have fit. He said the women often got weak and fell sick. I started to shiver. We moved to a different area, one where he said the men were kept, separate from the women. That's when I saw the old man, standing behind us, a little bit apart from everyone else. He didn't look like the other people in the tour group. He was wearing a heavy white lappa with one corner thrown over his shoulder; his hair was gray, he had wrinkles, and his feet were bare. He looked so sad, as if he were about to cry. I grabbed my mom's hand; I wanted her to look around at him, but she just pulled me closer to her. I didn't say anything. I didn't want to open my mouth, didn't want to breathe the air in that place. I wanted to go home. I looked back again and the man was still there. I squeezed my eyes shut and stumbled forward, holding on to my mom. When I opened my eyes and looked back again, he was gone. At last, we came out of the dungeons and I gulped in the salty ocean air and felt a little bit better. Aunty Nana-Yaa saw my face and touched my shoulder. She said something to my mom, I couldn't make it out, and my mom nodded. We all stayed quiet, as if the darkness of the dungeons had followed us outside and there was so much to say about it, but no one knew how to find the words.

After a long time, my mom said, "Nonso, the Benya Lagoon is nearby. Let's go there and you can swim and then we'll eat something and go back to Accra, okay?"

I didn't feel hungry at all, but I nodded, relieved that we would be heading far away from the dungeons. We got to the lagoon, where the water was a greenish blue and it looked so beautiful, so different from the place we had just left. I had a swimsuit on under my clothes because my mother had told me that we might go swimming, if we had enough time. I took off my jeans and T-shirt once we got to the beach and headed into the water. The water covered my ankles, then my knees. I lay flat on my back, floating and looking up at the sky. When I felt a little better, I flipped over and dog paddled away from my mom and her friend. The lagoon got deeper, and when I looked down I saw a flash of white. I slowed down to look closer and there he was, the sad old man in the white lappa from the dungeons. He was in trouble and I knew I had to save him. I took in a deep breath and dove deep down; I'd grab his lappa and then get my hand around his neck and kick my way to the shore. I couldn't seem to reach him, though, no matter how hard I swam; something seemed to be sucking him away from me. I don't remember what happened next, but somehow I was on the beach, coughing and retching, and my mother was holding me. She was crying so hard her body was shuddering. I tried to tell her that I was fine, that we had to go back and get the old man.

"What old man?" she said.

"The old man from the dungeons," I said, frantic. "He's going to drown if we don't get him."

She gave me a weird look. I said, "He was in the water right there in the lagoon. Mummy, he looks so sad; we have to help him."

"Nonso," she said gently. "There's nobody in the lagoon. You almost drowned, we had to save *you*. You're not going back in there."

"But I saw . . ."

"You're not going back in there."

Aunty Nana-Yaa squatted down beside me. She said, "Nonso, you've had quite a day today, and your mom and I were so worried. We should head home. I can make some more of the fried plantain and kontombre you had yesterday. Wouldn't you like that?"

I looked at both of them and realized that they were watching me very carefully.

"You didn't see him?"

"Nonso, there was no one else there," my mother said again, this time with a look of fear on her face. I noticed that her eyes were red and puffy. It occurred to me that I was scaring her.

I knew what I'd seen in the castle and I knew I'd seen the same old man in the water, but I'd never seen my mother cry before. I didn't remember them grabbing me out of the water, didn't remember how I got from the water back to land, so I nodded my head and didn't say anything more. Nothing on the drive from Elmina back to Accra. Nothing on the flight from Accra to Ibadan. Nothing on the drive from the airport to our house on Sankore Avenue.

I know what I saw.

GOODY GOODY

1997
DEOLA

They burned all her pictures one by one and left me nothing. Nothing. Her baby pictures, all fat cheeks, huge eyes and football belly, impossibly tiny fingers and curled toes. Her naming ceremony picture, her mouth a startled circle just after I pinched her, so we'd have at least one picture of her with her eyes wide open (she didn't even cry, just went back to sleep after the shot). The Christmas and Easter pictures where we sat in a row in our best clothes, her father and I beaming proudly, our four children flanking us, Solape always at my right-hand side. The one I took myself on visiting day at Federal Government Girls College, Fiditi, with Aisha, Nonso, and Remi holding Solape up as she lay sideways, safe in their grasp, everyone facing the camera and laughing, after gorging themselves on my jollof rice.

"Solape, your mom makes the best jollof," I remember Aisha saying to her as the other two nodded. I couldn't hold back the smile that stretched out my lips, though I pretended I couldn't hear, their reward more rice heaped on their plates.

Solape was the smallest of the four, the only one they could carry that way. The other girls' nickname for her was No Jagbaja, because her favorite saying was "Please, no jag-bajantis," when she felt that someone was talking rubbish.

I always wanted a daughter, knew deep down that daughters would take the best care of me in my old age, if all else failed. Boys mean well but they are clueless about the little things, and if they bring home a woman who doesn't like you, forget it. I worried when I had three boys after Solape; I wanted another girl, but none came. Then my periods stopped and that was that. There would be no fifth child.

I cried for four months straight after her funeral, cried until my husband went from cradling me to scolding me.

"You will end up in hospital if you keep doing this every day. Deola, please, please stop. I miss her too. We all miss her."

I heard his distress and nodded, tried to hold the tears in, but they leaked out the sides of my eyes and flowed freely down my face. They weren't done with me yet; I could do nothing to stop them.

Five months after the funeral, I felt well enough to go visit my best friend, Bisi, and my husband encouraged me to do so, to leave the house whose four walls had been my cocoon.

"Mama Diran," Bisi said when I arrived, folding me into her arms. It still startled me to hear that name. Just six months prior, I was Mama Solape. The first time I heard someone call me Mama Diran was a week after we learned she was gone. It took all the energy out of me—I had to sit down when I heard it. I wasn't ready. I'm still not ready, all these years later, but now I understand that so many of the things we do are to keep everyone else comfortable and sane, to keep the madman gibbering between our ears safely locked in. I'm careful, very careful to make sure no one else hears him.

I spent two hours with Bisi and finally was able to keep the things that had been haunting me, that had been on a steady replay loop, over and over and over, out of my mind. "Was she afraid? Did she call for me? Did the police officers mock her when she told them she needed air, that she couldn't breathe?"

When I got home, I noticed it immediately, the family portrait on the wall just opposite the entryway was gone. I felt a sense of dread. It was worse than I thought. Much worse. My husband cried for the second time since we got married, the second time since we got the news. I didn't care, I would have torn him apart with my bare hands if I wasn't five foot one and he six feet.

I screamed at him as I beat my hands against his chest. "You will never, ever understand. You have your sons. You have your sons and I have no daughter."

The look of anguish on his face stopped me in my tracks. "What are you saying? Are they not your sons too? Was Solape not my daughter?"

Confused, I started to mumble, "That's not what I'm saying. You know what I mean . . ."

"No, I'm not sure I do. I'm sorry, but this has got to stop. You have to pull yourself together. Deola, you're frightening me and the boys, too."

After he said that, I calmed down. I knew he meant well, knew he was scared for me, but I've never forgiven him. He didn't burn them himself but he let in those who did and showed them what to torch. So stupid. You can't burn out the memories, the images etched into my brain. I'll always see her the way I want to. No one can take that away from me.

———

I heard that the girls were at the funeral, but of course, Solape's father and I weren't there. You don't go to bury your only daughter. No parents should be at the funeral of their child. The first time I remember the girls visiting me was two years after but it's possible that they showed up even before then. It's the time I remember most vividly. They came to the house all together, and at first there was this awkward and stilted conversation. I asked about their mothers, their fathers, their sisters and brothers. I offered them food, but they'd eaten. I offered them cold Fanta and Coca-Cola, and finally, they said yes. Solape's father wasn't home. He was rarely home those days and even if he had been, he'd probably have stayed in the confines of our bedroom. He resented the fact that they were still here and she wasn't. He knew it wasn't right but he couldn't help himself, and when he told me that, I said I felt the opposite. She talked about them nonstop when she was on break—it made my heart lighter to know she had such good friends, that she chose wisely, because here they were years later, not forgetting. It was Aisha who took us from clumsy platitudes to something real.

Solape used to steal from my purse when she was in primary school. One naira here, fifty kobo there. We didn't have a househelp back then, I was pregnant with my last child, and the other two boys were too young to know what to do with money at that point. I knew it had to be her. I knew why. I didn't let them eat sweets, wouldn't give her money to buy them.

"Your teeth will be rotten," I said each time she asked. Eventually she nodded and stopped asking. Then I noticed these small amounts missing from my purse. Not every day. More like every two weeks or so. One day I found some discarded Goody Goody and Trebor wrappers stuffed under her mattress. Don't ask me why I was looking under her mattress, I wasn't snooping, just decided to change her sheets and there they were. I'd taught her to make her bed to prepare her for boarding school, so I left things the way they were, backed out of her room, and didn't say anything to her when she got back from school, her face bright with excitement because she scored ten out of ten on her math test. She loved math but she also loved to read. Anything and everything—Pacesetters, mysteries, you name it, she read it and I let her. I let her ignore her chores sometimes because she was so absorbed in those books and it made me feel good that my daughter loved books so much, that she would be the first woman in my family to go to university.

Aisha said Solape wanted to tell me about the money. It bothered her and she wanted to say something because I was always so proud of her, but she didn't know how I would react. She was waiting until she got to form five to tell me because maybe then we could laugh about it, but she'd felt so guilty after taking money from my purse.

"Stealing," I said.

Aisha went quiet. Remi averted her eyes and said, "Solape knew it was wrong taking money from your purse, but she loved Goody Goody so much. It was . . . she was never allowed to have any."

Solape told Aisha, Remi, and Nonso about it and they asked her whether I'd ever said anything about missing money. She said no.

Nonso, smart girl that she was, told her, "Your mom probably knows."

Solape said, "No, if she did, she'd beat me, one for taking money from her purse without asking and two for eating sweets."

Nonso guessed right, though. I don't know why I never confronted Solape about it. I was half-amused, a little disappointed, but in primary six, she stopped taking money from my purse and then there was no point dwelling on it. Talking to the three of them that day, I realized that I could bring up how she cursed at me sometimes, mix in the bad with the good. Solape wasn't a saint, just a young girl with so much ambition and so much living to do. They weren't afraid to say her name, weren't afraid I was fragile or I'd break because they didn't see me during those early days. They never saw me cry. I wanted details. I wanted to know everything about how they lived in boarding school, what she thought of the food, how much she missed me, her father, her brothers. What they fought about, laughed about. I wanted to know this daughter of mine, see her through her friends' eyes. I knew her to be fierce, determined—I mean she knew she wanted to go to university when she was just four years old. Her uncle had a land dispute and the rest of the family decided to show up in court to support him and I took Solape with me; I'm not sure why. The judge was a forty-something-year-old woman in long black robes and a ridiculous white wig; she looked stern but forgiving, like Oya in human form. Solape watched her all afternoon and then announced that she was going to be a lawyer and then a judge. She never forgot that judge. I looked at Solape that day and thought about my childhood classmates. Maybe they were lawyers and judges and doctors now. I did very well in the school in my small town but most of the time I came fourth in my class; there were two girls and one boy who did better. Sometimes I switched with the boy for third place, but usually he beat me. One term, I came second and I was on a cloud of joy for two days; my mother gave me my own piece of meat as a reward, a fat chicken drumstick all to myself, instead of the chicken feet that us kids usually shared. I wanted to go to university but the scholarships in my town were only for those who came first, second, and third overall. I was fourth. Fourth and my father said he didn't have the money, so I never went. Fourth. It ate at me for years, but after I had Solape, I realized that she could do everything I didn't get a chance to do. She would be a lawyer. She would go to university, because I married a man who went and who wanted that for his children as much as I did. Even though I never studied at a university, I found my own way; I made enough money feeding people at my buka, Come Chop, that it didn't even matter whether my husband was able to pay fees, because I could. My father couldn't or wouldn't, but I could.

———

They come to visit me every few years. Aisha, Nonso, and Remi, the quiet one. When they all ended up in America, I thought that was it, but no. I'd get the occasional phone call on her birthday and a gift now and then, but every few years, when they are in

Nigeria, they come to visit. Always together. They let me know they were coming this year, so I told them to visit me today, the day that I'm opening my new restaurant, moving Come Chop to a new location not far from the old kiosk. No more customers jockeying for space at the two long wooden tables and benches out front. It will be indoors now, a big space with a kitchen in the back and ten wooden tables that can fit fifty customers comfortably. I'm sure they noticed that it coincides with her twenty-sixth birthday. It's been a long time coming, and I'm happy that it's here and it's with their help. I saved all the gift money Aisha and Remi and Nonso sent, the dollars, and along with the profit from my buka, it built up over the years and now here I am. Today is going to be a special day. I had a professional sign maker create a new sign, a new name to go with the new location and expanded menu, it's covered up in the front and I'm going to unveil it today. We're opening at eleven with a prayer from my pastor and I've told all my old customers where to find us.

I see Remi first and then the three of them are surrounding me, dipping to the floor in greeting, and next come the hugs. Solape's father took the day off today so they greet him, too, and this time he smiles and doesn't head for the back to avoid them. The pastor says the prayer and my belly is queasy, but I let everyone know to make their way out front, where there's a heavy cloth covering the new sign. I stand next to my husband, motion to the new waiter and waitress to pull off the cloth, and then I hear a shuddering sigh come from Solape's father. I don't look at him yet, I can't look at him, so I just stare at the sign, which proclaims in humongous letters:

MAMA SOLAPE'S BUKATERIA!

He turns to me and, to my surprise, there's a smile on his face, not a scowl, and he gathers me into his arms, his back to the sign. I start to cry a little, from relief and joy, the anxiety that had gathered, constricting my lungs, now easing.

I'm facing the front of the new restaurant when I see Solape's face in one of the windows, a cheeky grin on it, like the one she had when she was six and broke something I'd told her not to touch and I was going to whip her but she ran to her father, and he lifted her up, away from me to safety.

He said, "Please leave her, she's sorry, she didn't do it on purpose, can't you see she's sorry?" right as she stuck out her tongue at me.

I was so angry that day. Today, I return the smile. I peer closer at the window but now it's just my face staring back at me. I know she was there, smiling her approval at the restaurant name, at the gathering, at her friends, at the fact that I've never forgotten, will never forget.

CZEKOLADA

2003
AISHA

The walk from my hotel to Krakow's main market square took
fifteen minutes. I wouldn't normally have set off alone, but the
morning I met Todd, I was bored and trying to stop thinking about Andrew, my ex. Walking seemed like a good way
to distract myself. It was a sunny July morning in 2003 and
my friend Sylwia had gotten married in Krakow the day before. The rest of the wedding party was sleeping off the vodka
from the reception. Midway through the toasts, I'd replaced
the vodka in my shot glass with water, so I had myself to blame
for being the lone person up bright and early.

I decided to kill time until the rest of the wedding party
woke up by heading out to pick up postcard stamps from the

tourist information center in the square. There were very few people walking around, probably because nearly everyone was already at work. The day was almost too perfect; a clear, cloud-resistant blue sky and a cool breeze fluttering through kept the rising summer heat from biting.

I got to a semideserted stretch. It was just me and a teenage girl half a block away. She was dressed in tight blue jeans and a pink tank top, taking a smoke in front of an old five-story brick apartment building. As I drew closer, I saw that she had an unfortunate face: narrow at the top but filled out toward the middle with huge cheeks that brought to mind a ruminating camel. She couldn't have been more than fifteen but the pancake makeup on her face made her look much older. She turned to me as I approached and, with a mischievous expression on her face, broke into a loud song in Polish. I wasn't sure exactly what she was singing but I did catch the word czekolada several times. Chocolate. Chocolate. Chocolate. She repeated the word again and again. She was watching me carefully to gauge my reaction, eyes glinting with anticipation. I felt the knot that had untwisted after I left the wedding reception re-forming in the pit of my stomach. I hated feeling that tension build up inside of me, so I stretched my mouth wide and extended my middle finger to show my full appreciation of her vocal talent. She looked shocked for a moment, then let a tinkling laugh ring out, her expression now more admiring than impish. She'd just wanted to get a rise out of me and she had. Relieved that that's all it was, I waved goodbye and she waved back. I wasn't sure how long she'd stay friendly, so I stepped up my pace, hoping to get to the square quicker.

———

I'd read somewhere, can't remember where, that Krakow's main market square could hold three thousand soldiers standing side by side. As I walked through it, I wasn't sure that was true, but it really didn't matter—the sheer expanse of the square was awe-inspiring, almost overwhelming, and yet the historic buildings at its center and perimeter had a charm that lifted my spirits and brought a smile to my face. Halfway across the square, I stopped to stare at a group of teenagers break-dancing in front of Adam Mickiewicz's statue, tinny hip-hop blasting from a small boom box at the statue's base. I'd never thought staccato gangsta rhymes and monuments to dead poets belonged together, but watching them gyrate, it all made sense. One teen performed an impressive series of flips, ending in a one-handed handstand. I wished I had my digital camera on me to record his feat but I'd left it in my hotel room. None of my friends back home would believe this without hard evidence.

Who knew hip-hop would follow me, spread through Krakow like the queasiness that came with breakfast as the bleep-free hook of Noreaga's "Nothin'" floated over my table. I'd never heard the uncensored version before, don't think a restaurant stateside would have dared play it. I swallowed each "nigga" with a sip of hot chocolate, my stomach roiling as the words stacked up, refusing to dissolve in acid. In New York or Boston, I'd bop my head to the beat, shake my shoulders a little, ignorant of just what the bleeped words were. Here, at breakfast, I shook my head from side to side, knowing no one else understood the lyrics, hoping no one would decide to mouth them. "Thanks a lot, N.O.R.E.," I'd whispered under my breath.

Watching the break-dancers, I wondered whether they understood the songs they were dancing to. Ten minutes later, I remembered I still hadn't purchased the stamps. Turning away from the statue, I headed toward the tourist center.

Five workers sat behind a series of tables and a kiosk. Their eyes begged for something, anything remotely interesting to come into view. Unfortunately, I wasn't it. I checked my travel dictionary, preparing to point to the appropriate phrase and mime buying stamps. My Polish vocabulary was limited to "dzien dobry" and "dzjiekuje" and I already knew "hello" and "thank you" would only get me so far.

A female worker dragged her eyes away from her fuchsia-colored nails and asked in flawless English, "What is it you need?"

"Postcard stamps for the U.S."

She gestured to a sandy-haired man behind the glass window. I made my way over to him.

"How can I help you?" He had a clipped British accent.

I made my purchase and applied the stamps and airmail stickers, obscuring half the information I'd written but figuring my friends would be happy to receive something from Poland, never mind whether they could read it.

I read over my message to Nonso. It was, word for word, the same as the one to Remi, my other best friend:

> Had so much fun at Sylwia's wedding yesterday! Visited Zakopane, Andrew's hometown, last week. Don't be alarmed, I just wanted to see what kind of town birthed the ClingOn, but looks like he caught whatever he did in Chicago. Zakopane was beautiful and I sure got a lot of attention. Tell you all about it when I get back.
>
> Love,
> Aisha

The ClingOn was my ex-boyfriend, Andrzej, who left the ski resort town of Zakopane for Chicago at the age of six. He started calling himself Andrew as soon as he could string ten English words together. In all honesty, I accepted Sylwia's wedding invitation because I wanted to know more about where Andrew came from.

Last week, Sylwia said her future in-laws had asked to visit Zakopane. I went with them. The ski slopes were a lush green, the town teeming with July hikers and campers. On our walk, a gaggle of eight-year-old boys approached us.

"Hi," one of them said, looking right at me. His hair was the same pale lemon-juice shade as Andrew's, his eyes the color of a cloudless sky at midday.

"Hi," I said back, smiling. "How are you today?"

The boys stared at one another, mouths widening into large O's, and started to giggle.

"I fine," said the ringleader, tapping his chest proudly as he reached the limits of his English. They followed us for a while, echoing *hi* and *hello*.

Sylwia said, "You're a hit!"

I felt a tiny ball of anxiety form in the base of my throat. I laughed, loudly, but that didn't dislodge it. We lost the boys after a while, but not the blatant stares.

"I guess this is different from Paris or London." I'd traveled through both cities and never attracted any attention.

"You guess right," Sylwia said.

She and the others decided to climb up a steep hill. I was feeling too lazy to join in, so I waited for them at its base. Not long after their figures became ant-like in the distance, an old man carrying what I assumed was his granddaughter stopped in front of me, beaming. He said something in Polish I didn't understand, raising the child up so she could see me.

I said, "She's beautiful, isn't she?"

He smiled even wider, extending his arms in my direction, until she was practically in my face. Not knowing the Polish words for "I don't have a maternal bone in my body," I grasped the baby awkwardly under her shoulders. As I cooed to her softly, she stared up at me with big brown unblinking eyes, totally unperturbed to be out of her grandpa's arms. After a minute or two, she opened her mouth in a wide, uvula-baring yawn, rubbing her right eye with one tiny fist.

"You're sleepy, huh? What's her name?" I asked, looking at her grandfather but knowing he wouldn't understand a word.

He said something in reply and we grinned at each other like idiots in the balmy orange silence. I liked the crinkles at the corners of his eyes, the deep grooves beside his mouth that made it clear he laughed a lot.

"It's funny how you can get along with someone when you don't even speak the same language," I said.

He smiled wider, and after a few minutes, gestured for the baby. I handed her back and he bowed slightly as they left.

When Sylwia and the others came back down, I said, "So this is Andrew's hometown."

"Aisha, you okay?" she said, a look of concern on her face.

"Never been better," I said. "Let's go back to Krakow."

———

The first time I saw Andrew, I was attending a meditation class in Boston. I was stressed out about my job, and an acquaintance from work had told me that meditation was a good way to deal with it. At the first meeting, we sat in a circle and said our names and intentions for the class. Andrew was directly opposite me, seated next to a girl I assumed was his girlfriend because of the way she'd punched his arm and laughed repeatedly as they talked before the instructor came in. He had a crew cut, chiseled cheekbones softened by slight stubble, and surprisingly full lips. He smiled a lot that day, and when he did, it made me want to cup his face in my hands, kiss him long and hard. The sister code ingrained in me from attending an all-girls boarding school meant that I avoided anything that could be construed as coming on to another woman's man. It didn't matter whether I knew the woman in question. In spite of my attraction, I'd completely tuned him out thirty minutes into class.

The next few classes, I noticed Andrew stealing glances at me and laughed to myself. *Your girlfriend is going to lock your eyeballs up in her purse if you're not more discreet*, I thought. When we were supposed to have our eyes closed during metta, I felt his gaze move from my forehead to my cheeks, my lips, my chin. I opened my eyes and raised an eyebrow. He went scarlet but didn't look away, so I shook my head and went back to reciting my mantras. The week of our second-to-last class, he plonked himself down right next to me. I looked around but didn't see his girlfriend.

At the end of the class he said, "Hey, Aisha, I was thinking that maybe we could be in the same sitting group to keep up practice after class ends, like Gary suggested." Gary was the meditation instructor.

I liked the way his breath caught slightly as he spoke my name but ignored the question buried in his statement. "Your girlfriend is not in class today," I said, making a show of looking around. "Hope she's feeling okay."

"Who?" He looked puzzled for a minute. "Do you mean Cheryl? She's my roommate, not my girlfriend. She got me to take this class with her because her boyfriend thinks meditation is woo."

"Oh," I said. Then I blurted out, "Yeah, I wondered why she didn't knock your head off, the way you kept staring—" and then stopped myself.

Andrew burst out laughing. "Ah, you noticed."

———

He asked me out right after the last class, his roommate in the background, trying to keep her distance *and* listen in to our conversation without seeming too obvious, a wide grin on her face once I said, "Sure, why not?"

He took me to a Thai restaurant in Boston, an Afghan restaurant in Cambridge, and for Brazilian food in Framingham. We visited the Boston Harbor Islands, making out in the cool, damp shadows of Fort Warren, our picnic lunch forgotten. We went bowling with Cheryl and her boyfriend. For our sixth date, I decided to invite him over for dinner on a Saturday. We made love in every corner of the apartment and fell asleep, exhausted, on the floor of the living room in front of the TV.

One year later, Andrew and I had moved in together. I bought him a copy of *The Famished Road* on a Friday and he finished reading it that same weekend. He got me to appreciate *The Master and Margarita*—we took turns reading that aloud to each other and Andrew did voices, inventing crazy accents that left me in hiccups from laughing so hard. We visited Paris (his idea) and explored Zanzibar (mine). Every month we tried out a new recipe, chopping, sautéing, and stirring ingredients together in our cozy kitchen, then inviting friends over to share. We talked seriously about getting married.

Then, two years after we'd made a home together, Andrew lost his job. He was very disciplined when it came to finances; before him, I'd never dated anyone who had a few years' worth of living expenses in an emergency savings account. I knew he'd find a new job and told him to take some time to relax and just enjoy living. But he couldn't. I'd never realized until then how much he'd let work define his very being, his sense of value and worth. We didn't go out to eat anymore. He didn't seem interested in the books I suggested and no longer had any to recommend to me. He gave up his cell phone and stopped taking his friends' calls. He didn't want them over for dinner because he couldn't bear talking about his job prospects. Travel was out of the question because Andrew was afraid it would deplete his savings and too proud to let me pay for trips. I came home from work to find him sprawled out on the couch in his PJs, watching TV or eating potato chips, dirty dishes in the sink, our bed unmade, clothes strewn about the apartment floor. He was becoming a living, breathing cliché right in front of me, so I made it my mission to show him how much he still had to offer. I talked to him about tutoring kids while he waited for the interviews to roll in. I hugged him, gave him massages. Nothing I did was enough.

I had applied to law school before he got laid off, partly to get away from the job I disliked so much (I'd stopped meditating and just couldn't deal with it anymore). The acceptance letter came, thick and weighty with the promise of a new future, a better life, and I was ecstatic.

Andrew said to me, "Is this what you really want, Aisha?"

My skin prickled as I pushed his words from my mind. "What do you mean?" I said. "You can't be happy for me?"

"If it's what you really want, then I'm happy for you," he said softly, but I heard it, that subtle inflection he couldn't keep from his voice when he disapproved of something, and I lost it.

I jabbed him in the chest, yelling as he walked backward. "You're not going to bring me down with you, you hear me? I'm trying to make things better and you won't let me. I'm sick of it."

Andrew was ashen, shaking. "Aisha, I'm sorry. I know I've been in a bad way. I can see that. I know you don't mean what you just said. And you and I both know that you don't really want to go to law school."

His words seared into my core and the loathing I felt for him in that moment was new, alien. I moved out of our apartment eight weeks after I started law school and spent half a semester sleeping on Sylwia's couch before I found my own place.

Andrew found out my new number after I moved from Sylwia's to my own apartment. He leaves me a message once a week to say hello, fill me in on his new job, ask me how I'm doing, and let me know how much he misses me. I listen and hit SAVE. Sometimes I'll replay his messages several times, but I never call back.

———

I placed the remaining stamps and stickers on the seventh postcard. I was feeling an odd tingling sensation on my right side. After a moment or two, I pinpointed its cause: a tall guy with a bushy coffee-colored beard gazing at me. I was still unnerved by the occasional curious stares my brown skin evoked here, so I turned back quickly to the postcards. Then I processed this fact: the guy with the brown beard staring at me was wearing knee-length shorts, sneakers, and a white long-sleeved T-shirt with a faded Boston Red Sox logo, and carrying a backpack. Very unlikely to be a Krakovian. He moved closer.

"Where do the airmail stickers go on the postcards?" The accent was definitely New England.

I felt a rush of relief and gratitude on hearing his accent and had to fight an insane urge to hug him. Finally, someone who asked a question I could handle and didn't leave me feeling like some exotic freak. I couldn't help smiling. "Below the address line," I replied. He'd made the same mistake as I had in writing out the postcard's message before factoring in the myriad stamps and stickers that would need to adorn it.

"Where are you from?" I asked him. He reminded me of Andrew, though they looked nothing alike. It was something about the way he tilted his head slightly to one side when he talked.

"Connecticut." He grinned. "How about you?"

I gave the abbreviated version. "I'm visiting from Boston."

"Boston!" His smile widened. "I guessed you were visiting from the States." Up close, he looked like a college student.

"Cambridge, actually," I said. "Do you go to school in Boston?"

"I graduated from Bates College in Maine last year. You?"

"I'm just about to start my second year of law school. I was done with college in '94." If he graduated last year, I had nine years on this kid.

His eyes widened slightly.

"So what brings you to Krakow?" I asked as we both headed out to find a postbox for our stamped postcards.

"Oh, been traveling through Eastern Europe. Yesterday, I came in from Budapest, which was awesome. I'm headed for Romania the day after tomorrow." His fingers searched for a patch of skin somewhere beneath the beard and scratched furiously. "What brings you to Krakow?"

I shook off mental images of miniature bird nests being violently dislodged from the thatch of facial hair. "A friend's wedding. It started at four p.m. yesterday and was supposed to go on until eight this morning, though I called it quits by two a.m."

"How come?"

I told him how the reception party split into those who spoke English and those who spoke mostly Polish, and that my friend Sylwia had warned me I'd get asked to dance quite a bit by the Polish men because I was black. I was chatting with someone who knew the groom from his college days in Virginia, when a huge guy interrupted, pointing at me: "You. Dance. Me. Now!" It sounded more like an order than a request, and although I knew that was because he didn't speak much English, he looked like someone I didn't want to piss off. I noticed a petite woman and a little boy trailing the man. "My wife, my son," he said. He started twirling me around while she broke out the camera, grinning and clicking away.

Weird enough, but the end of the party came for me when another guy cut in, and when I complimented him on his swing dancing, picked me up and flipped me over like I weighed no more than a matchstick. One strap of my dress snapped, all the vodka, wine, mutton, cabbage, chicken, and potatoes we'd had for the numerous wedding dinner meals started to reverse course, and I fled to my room.

It felt good to talk to someone about how rattled I'd been by what had happened at the reception. He scratched at his arm as I spoke, his brow furrowed. "Sounds like quite a wedding party, aggressive dance requests, dress destruction, and all. How do you know the couple?"

"The bride and I are law school classmates. She let me camp out on her couch rent-free for two months—I had to be at her wedding." I got a little embarrassed because I'd been going on and on about the wedding and hadn't asked him much about himself. "What's your strangest travel experience so far?"

He told me he'd boarded a train that he thought was heading toward Krakow early yesterday morning and fallen asleep. When he woke up a few hours later, he found out that the car he was in had been detached from the original engine while he was sleeping and reattached to a locomotive heading elsewhere. He eventually found a guy who spoke enough English to help him sort things out when they got to the next station.

"You're lucky you found someone you could explain your situation to," I said.

"I know," he said. "He's coming to visit me in Connecticut next year."

"Ah. Getting lost on trains is a great way to make friends, huh?" I smiled.

"You can say that again." He motioned to one of the many cafés dotting the square. "You want to get something to drink?"

"Sure," I said. "But first I need to buy some gifts for my two best friends. I could use some help picking out something."

"I guess I'll tag along, then," he said.

We moved from one jewelry stall to another in the Sukiennice, a large rectangular building with beautiful Italian arches at the center of the square.

I picked up a green amber bracelet for Remi, brown amber teardrop earrings for Nonso, and a silver necklace with a green amber pendant for myself.

"Dzjiekuje," I told the seller once I'd made my purchase.

Surprised, she exclaimed, "You speak Polish?"

"That and two other words."

We both laughed.

"You have good accent," she said.

As we headed for a café with comfortable outdoor seating, I realized that we'd been talking all this time and hadn't even exchanged names.

"Aisha." I pointed to myself, smiling. "By the way."

"Todd." He grinned back.

We ordered two tall glasses of Zywiec beer and a margherita pizza and settled into some sturdy wicker chairs with a view of St. Mary's Basilica. We watched other tourists get carriage rides around the square, the horses clip-clopping despondently, as if wondering whether this was all an equine life had to offer.

I looked away from the horses and asked Todd, "What's the one place you haven't yet visited but would like to?"

"Africa," he said, without missing a beat.

"For a safari," I said. The words spilled from my mouth before I could stuff them back in. They were more accusation than question. I wondered why I'd said them.

Something about my tone made him lean forward, his eyes anxious, the pupils strangely dilated. "My family lived in Amherst for nine years. Our neighbors were from Ghana. Their oldest son was my best friend all through grade school. We still keep in touch. I plan to visit Ghana with him someday."

Todd swept the space between us with his fingers as he spoke, like he was brushing away some rank odor.

I gave him what I hoped was a reassuring smile. "I'm sorry, don't know why I said that. What's your friend's name?"

"Quasi," he said, scratching his left arm.

"Kwesi, not Kwazee," I said, correcting him before I could stop myself. "He isn't a false friend, is he?" I was on a roll with the verbal diarrhea.

Todd smiled at my lame joke—he'd probably made a decision to remain outwardly unruffled by anything I said. "Kwaysee," he repeated. "Like his mom says it. All his friends call him Quasi, though. He doesn't mind. How come you pronounce it so well?"

"I'm from Nigeria," I said. "Ghana's two countries away and that's a common name."

"But you don't have an accent." He took a swig of his beer.

"I'm an accent chameleon," I said. "My mom is African-American and my dad's Nigerian. I learned to speak to my mom in her accent and to my dad in his, and now I'm used to it. I'd speak English with a Polish accent if I stayed here two more weeks."

Smiling, he pressed his right hand down on the café table. "A Nigerian-American-Polish accent. That I'd love to hear."

I noticed then that he had beautiful hands; long and perfectly tapered, though the oval nails were a bit dirty.

"How come you're backpacking across Eastern Europe by yourself?" I asked.

He gave me a serious look and said, "I broke up with my girlfriend three months ago. I guess I'm looking for a replacement."

I squirmed a little in my seat. "How's the search going?"

"Pretty good so far." The corners of his mouth turned up and he seemed delighted at my discomfort.

"How long were the two of you together?"

"Ten months. It wasn't really going anywhere, though. Is your boyfriend also here in Krakow?"

"We split up a little while ago. Frankly, I'm not in a hurry to lose my freedom again."

"That bad, huh?" Todd scratched at his neck as I spoke.

"We lived together for two years and basically got on each other's last nerve." I sipped my beer so I wouldn't have to say more.

———

Todd and I had downed a couple of beers talking about family, friends, and travel. I paid my half of the tab as Todd talked about his trip to Budapest. Soon it was time to find a restroom, and I retrieved my backpack from its resting place under the café table to extract a few coins. This was the first city I'd been to that had monitors at every public restroom. There was a charge of one zloty per visit.

"So what are you doing tomorrow?" Todd asked when I returned.

"A group of us from the wedding are going to check out the salt mines."

He rocked backward in his chair, scratched his right arm. "I think I'll check that out at some point. Probably not on this visit, though."

I looked at my watch. "I should get going—I'm supposed to meet with the other wedding guests soon. Want to join us for dinner later on?"

Todd shook his head regretfully. "I should probably head out to Wawel Castle, see more of the Krakow sights; I'm leaving for Romania in a day. Where are you staying?"

"In Kazimierz."

He smiled. "Good choice. I hear they have some new klezmer groups playing there. The fashionable thing for young Polish musicians with a conscience. Or something."

"I heard that too, and I'm curious enough to check it out while we're here."

"Mmm," he said. "You know, we should keep in touch."

I thought about the German couple I met in Brazil, the Australian I hung out with while at a youth hostel in South Africa, the Nebraskan I literally bumped into at the British Museum while marveling at the transported wonders of Egypt. All amazing people I swore I'd keep in touch and meet up with again someplace. It never happened.

"Sure," I said, "we should meet up in Boston."

"Sounds like a plan."

As we exchanged addresses and phone numbers, a young Rom man walked up to the table with wristwatches for sale. I'd noticed him earlier trying to sell them on the other side of the square. Todd shook his head with a smile, and the man moved on to the tourists at the next table.

"He looks so much like a friend I had in high school who died," Todd said. "Car accident." He looked down at the table. "I was driving." He said the last bit quietly but the words carried over clearly.

I gasped. "Oh my God, that must have been terrible."

Todd sighed, still looking at the young man, who was now four tables away. He said, "He'd been drinking but I was sober, which is why I took the wheel. It was his car, we weren't supposed to be out but we were. Rainy night and the brakes weren't working well. We skidded on a turn and hit a tree . . ." His voice went lower and lower. "He didn't make it. I was in the hospital for four months. They said it was the faulty brakes." He placed his hands on the table and looked down at them.

I put my right hand over his left, my eyes were blurry with tears. "I know exactly how you feel."

Todd looked up at me and said in a sharp tone, "How do I feel?"

I ignored the edge in his voice, said, "This is going to sound crazy, but I lost a friend in boarding school. Back in Nigeria."

"How?"

"I helped to plan a riot—we had a crazy principal we were trying to get rid of." I paused for a moment, trying to think of how to go on without unraveling; Nonso and Remi and I broke down every time we talked about that night, so we had avoided doing so for years. "Anyway, my friend Solape refused to join in but she got arrested and the police wouldn't take me in instead of her, even when I told them that I was involved and she wasn't.

"She died from an asthma attack. They didn't have her inhaler or even believe that she wasn't faking until it was too late."

"My God," Todd said. He slumped a little in his chair.

I leaned forward. "I've only told one other person this but the reason I'm going to law school is because I knew that she wanted to be a lawyer. I promised myself that I would try to do as many of the things that she'd wanted to do as I could." I shook my head. "When I told Andrew—that's my ex—he started telling me all this bullshit about how I couldn't live her life and it wasn't my fault."

Todd nodded his head like he understood exactly why that upset me. He looked down at the ground when he spoke. "I know you probably don't want to hear this right now, but your ex was right. Beating yourself up every day—I know what that is. It's not a life."

I wasn't upset the way I would have been if Andrew had said those same words. Todd *knew*. He knew. "Did you see your friend's parents after it happened?"

He sighed. "His mother came to the hospital to visit me two months after I regained consciousness. I have never forgotten the look of anguish as she told me that she forgave me and that it wasn't my fault. I see her sometimes when I sleep.

Always with her back to me, hunched over like she's crying, but I know it's her."

I gave him a hug and he hugged me back. We didn't say anything else to each other for a long time but I felt at peace. For the first time in a long time. I smiled at Todd. There was an odd look on his face, a mixture of sorrow and something else I couldn't quite place my finger on. He parted his lips as if he was about to say something, then pressed them back together.

I stood reluctantly. "I'd better get going now. It was really good meeting you. I'll be in touch when I get back to Boston."

This time I meant it.

Todd nodded, blinked, and the look that made me want to hug him again, tell him all would be right with the world, was gone.

———

There was a mild odor of horseshit in the air as I made my way back to the hotel in Kazimierz. I crossed over the trolley tracks that snaked throughout the city and thought about Todd. With his scruffy clothes, beard, and constant scratching, I'd never have looked at him twice in Boston, but I had to admit it was fun, no, not just that, cathartic, hanging out with him.

As I passed by Klezmer-Hois, which was not very far from the hotel, I got a strong craving for black currant juice. I'd developed quite a passion for it since visiting Krakow. I kept walking until I spotted a little grocery store.

When it was time to pay for the juice, I couldn't seem to find my wallet. At first I dug through the backpack, thinking it must be hidden under some of the junk I always carried around with me. Still no wallet. I left the juice on the counter as the old man at the register watched me, puzzled.

"My wallet is gone," I said in English.

He didn't understand me, smiled as he pointed to the bottle of juice. I shook my head violently, knowing I had no Polish words to express what was happening, and ran toward the hotel and my room.

I dumped the contents of the backpack on the room's narrow twin bed and sank to my knees as I picked up and examined each disgorged item, as if staring long and hard enough would cause the missing wallet to materialize. It stayed gone. Then I remembered leaving the backpack under the café table while I went to use the restroom. But Todd hardly seemed the type . . . I cut myself off before I could complete the thought. In a panic, I grabbed the slip of paper with his phone number and address in Connecticut and rushed down through the lobby. There was a pay phone at the corner I'd used for international phone calls. I had a new phone card in my shorts pocket. Soon a distant recording intoned, "At the customer's request, 203-555-9876 has been temporarily disconnected. No further information is available about 203-555-9876."

In a pouch fastened about my midsection I had my passport and my bank ATM card. I'd learned from a veteran backpacker friend not to store too much in my wallet while traveling. In spite of this sage advice, there was about $800 in it, all my credit cards, and 200 zloty.

How could I have been so stupid as to leave my backpack at the table, no matter how nice Todd seemed? I marveled at the nerve of the guy—after the restroom trip, we talked for more than a half hour and he didn't seem overly eager to cut the conversation short and split. What if I'd decided to order another beer or something? I decided not to mention how naïve I'd been to anyone else here for the wedding, then realized I'd need someone who spoke Polish to file a police report. Tears stung my eyes as I thought about all I'd lost.

I grabbed my backpack and hit the sidewalk running. Wherever Todd was, I was going to find him. I sprinted across the trolley tracks, ignoring odd looks from the few people parked on benches, chatting about their day. Soon I was back in the square. The break-dancers were still communing with Adam Mickiewicz. Todd wasn't near them. He'd said something about Wawel Castle, so I walked in that direction. Then I saw him ahead of me, moving past a small crowd gathered in front of a mime whose pale, ghostly arms were raised above her head. My hand on his shoulder was rough, and there was no mistaking the expression of surprise on his face.

"Where's my wallet?" I yelled.

"What wallet?" His voice sounded calm, concerned.

I lowered my voice, doubt sneaking through my veins and bringing down the temperature. "I left my wallet in my backpack when I went to use the restroom and now it's gone."

"So you think I took it?" His shoulders slumped as the words came out soft, quiet. I thought maybe I'd made a mistake but I was too confused to stop babbling.

"I didn't know what to think. I called the number you gave me and it was disconnected . . ." I took my hand off his shoulder.

"I have my number temporarily switched off while I'm traveling so I don't have to pay the full bill."

I blinked and looked down at my scuffed black loafers, mumbling, "I know it was in my backpack when I left the table . . ."

"I didn't realize you left your backpack under the table; I walked around a bit while you went to find a restroom. The guy with the wristwatches was standing at the table when I got back but I didn't think anything of it."

I was feeling more and more like an idiot with every passing minute. "Look, I'm sorry, I didn't know what to think," I said. I shook my head, at a loss for what to say next. "Todd, I'm sorry," I repeated.

"I'm not mad at you, you left the backpack near me so I can see why you might have thought what you did." He scratched his right arm.

There was a little trace of blood on his T-shirt sleeve at

the crook of the elbow. I wondered what kind of bugs bit him, he'd been scratching at his arms since I met him . . . Without stopping to think, I yanked up his right sleeve and there it was: a patchwork of scars, old needlemarks and fresh ones just scabbing over. My heart slamming against my ribs, I stepped back. I took in the wide, dilated pupils in the bright sunlight, the vacant stare. My bones felt leaden all of a sudden and an icy chill prickled the length of my spine; I wanted to squeeze my eyes shut for five minutes and reopen them with him gone because then he'd just be a nightmare my brain conjured up. That, I could manage.

"Please." It came out as a whisper. "Please give me back my wallet."

He didn't say anything, just reached into his backpack and pulled it out, and I took it from his hand.

I opened it up while he watched with those terrible, empty eyes. The cash was gone but all my credit cards were still there.

"Thank you." The words slipped out of my mouth unbidden. He just stood there, head hanging low, hugging his arms to his body. I began to feel scared for the first time. The crowd near the mime had dispersed. I turned from Todd, if that was even his real name, and sprinted back toward the main market square. When I looked over my shoulder once, he was moving away from me at a slow, unhurried pace, still heading toward Wawel Castle.

In the safety of the crowded square, I headed for a bank of

pay phones and placed a collect call. I didn't care what time it was in Boston.

"Aisha! Are you okay?" The voice sounded froglike from sleep but I was happy to hear it.

"Hi, Andrew," I said. "I'm in Krakow for Sylwia's wedding. Some Connecticut junkie just took my wallet but I chased him and got it back and the cash is missing but the credit cards are fine . . ."

"You chased him? What?" He was wide-awake now.

"I'm okay, I'm okay. He's gone, I'm in the square." There was a salty taste in my mouth from tears flowing freely down my face.

"You don't sound okay. Want me to come out there?"

I knew he would do it, too, get on the next flight if I said yes, and I felt grateful for that.

"No, no, don't do that. I'm fine."

"Where are the other people from the wedding?"

"In the hotel still sleeping," I said.

"I think you should head back there."

"Yeah, I probably should."

"Aisha?"

"Yes?"

"It's nice to hear from you."

"I went to Zakopane and saw a little boy that reminded me of you. You never told me it was so beautiful."

"I left too young to remember what it was like." He paused.

"You're smiling. I can hear it in your voice. How come you never return my calls?"

"Maybe because you were right," I said. "About law school. I hate it but I'm going to finish what I started." I started to wail then, the sobs racking my body.

"Aisha, I'll be on the next flight I can get out of Logan."

"You don't have to—" I stopped, my voice cracking.

"I want to," he said. "I'll see you tomorrow."

"What about your new job?"

"I'll tell them I have an emergency . . ." he said. "Aisha, just let me do this without nitpicking every detail."

"I'm sorry," I said. Then, "Thank you."

"I've missed you so much."

"God, Andrew, I've missed you, too." My stomach unclenched as I breathed in deeply, finally letting this truth seep into every pore. "More than you'll ever know."

LAST STOP, JIBOWU

2005

NONSO

Nonso's tailbone was sore from smashing into exposed seat springs. She shifted her weight onto her right side as her cousin Dibia coaxed his shuddering jalopy forward. They were heading to the bus stop where she'd catch a Delta Lines minibus from Anioma-Ukwu to Lagos. The exhaust pipe of Dibia's ancient Opel emitted a repulsive *put-put* sound as it spewed dark, foul smoke into the clear morning air. Earlier in the year, Nonso had wired Dibia a considerable amount of money from New York, enough to replace the Opel with a much newer car, if he'd chosen, but it seemed he'd found other, better uses for her generous gift.

Eleven people were waiting at the stop already, a few still bleary-eyed from cutting their sleep short to catch the first bus out. Nonso grabbed her Samsonite carry-on, aware of how obscenely clean it appeared in comparison with the bulging Ghana-must-go bags her fellow travelers had piled up in preparation for the trip. She removed a tattered American Airlines name tag from the suitcase's handle, stuffing it deep in her jeans pocket, next to the receipt for the minibus ride that said "Delta Lines, Anioma-Ukwu, Delta State. Destination: Jibowu, Lagos State. February 24, 2005." The driver loaded the minibus with bags, cassava tubers, two jerry cans filled with palm oil, giant snails strung together by their striped brown shells, and a large bunch of green plantains.

Nonso watched in bemusement as a fellow passenger's black plastic bag began to jerk and squawk. The owner, a fif-tyish woman in the middle of an animated conversation with a younger woman, paused mid-sentence, reached into the squawking bag, exposing the red-combed head and scrawny brown-feathered neck of a chicken, and gave it a sharp rap. The bird, dazed by this rude response, fell silent and still, meekly accepting a return to the now preferable confines of the bag. Across from the woman with the chicken, two little girls, five and six years at the most, were playing a clapping game. They sang in hushed tones so as not to arouse the wrath of their mother:

Babangida jump up, one naira fall
Uchenna take am, go buy chewing gum

Babangida call am, Uchenna come
Babangida slap am, Uchenna cry

Linking their skinny arms, they danced at this last bit, and Nonso smiled, remembering similar songs and games she'd played with friends as a child. She looked around to see an elderly woman waiting with a boy who looked about nine years old. He was staggering away from the woman with his arms stretched out, cursing her loudly any time she tried to help him. From their conversation, Nonso gathered his blindness was recent and somehow the woman's fault.

Nonso inhaled deeply, fascinated by her fellow passengers, now surer than ever that her decision to take a shared bus back to Lagos was the right one. Her older brother and his driver had brought her from Lagos to see her parents. He'd offered to send the driver to pick her up for her trip back but she declined. She wanted to experience Nigeria in a different way, free from the overprotective care of her family.

She gave Dibia a parting hug and climbed into the prized seat he'd negotiated for her; the rightmost front passenger seat next to the window. A young man engrossed in typing out a text message on his mobile phone sat between her and the driver. The other passengers gradually filed into the blue-and-white minibus emblazoned with the upside-down red triangles of the Delta Lines. Once the bus was full, the driver shut the passenger side sliding door and climbed into his seat.

He released the clutch just as a young couple made a mad dash for it.

"Please, sah, please!"

The bus seating space was now so crammed with passengers and their hand luggage, including the chicken, that Nonso feared the tires would explode.

"You go wait for the next one," the driver said to the couple and pulled away from the stop. Nonso felt bad for them; they might have to wait a few hours to leave.

As the driver eased the minibus onto a narrow street, a voice from the back yelled "Praise the Lord!" A chorus of Alleluias followed. Nonso sighed. She'd left Nigeria a lapsed Anglican and hadn't been to church much since her wedding day. Blatant public prayer hadn't been a thing seventeen years ago. She nervously twisted the gold wedding band on her left hand as the bus's self-selected preacher raised both arms and squeezed his eyes shut: "Lord grant us journey mercies, we know you are the alpha and the omega, Lord, cover us in the blood of Jesus, we ask you to bind all demons on the road and cast them far, far from us. Bind our enemies, Lord, so they will not succeed in harming us. Let us arrive safely at our destination, Lord . . ."

———

Three weeks earlier, as she sat in the two a.m. darkness of her Brooklyn apartment's living room, waiting for her husband,

Dwayne, to come home from work, Nonso had decided she needed a vacation. One that involved sucking down her mother's bitter-leaf soup and eating fried plantains, fried yam, and agidi for breakfast. The thought of yet another bowl of multigrain cereal and yogurt sickened her. She loathed the anemic January sunlight that struggled through the bedroom curtains in the morning. Seventeen years after she'd fled Nigeria's scalp-searing sun, there was nothing she wanted more than to roast herself in its orange heat.

The self-confident eighteen-year-old who'd left Nigeria all those years ago had morphed into a high-achieving, unhappy thirty-five-year-old. To cheer herself up, she mulled over the things acquired in seventeen years. Bachelor's degree in economics. Harvard MBA. Obscene salary from a top New York investment bank. Dwayne, whose hazel eyes made her insides smile the moment she laid eyes on him. She sighed, coiling her rope-thin body on the sofa. The problem was her last major acquisition, a terrifying sensation of being unmoored, disconnected from the things that had once brought her joy, coupled with a certainty that she would never be happy again.

She and Dwayne had wanted, no, expected, to have a child. They didn't discuss it much, it was just something they figured would happen once she stopped taking the pill. Two years after Nonso went off the pill, a diagnosis of premature ovarian failure ended that presumption. Dwayne said there were too many children in the world anyway; they could enjoy being godparents and an uncle and aunt and forgo the hassle of changing diapers and never sleeping through the night. They could travel whenever they wanted, wherever they wanted, and take risks that other couples couldn't. Nonso nodded but she secretly hoped that the doctors were wrong. Neither of them was particularly interested in adoption. Dwayne dove into work after the diagnosis, deciding to make partner at his law firm. Nonso took on more responsibilities at her investment banking job, volunteering for assignments that her colleagues who were parents wouldn't or couldn't take on. Then she noticed a numbness spreading in her chest as she staggered into the apartment from work in the wee hours of the morning on a Sunday. She thought a nine-to-five job might help ease it.

Her new job at a smaller bank slowed down its spread, but the numbness was a stubborn thing with a mind and a purpose all its own. It woke her up with questions like "Do you belong here?" and "Are you going to bury your bank account with you when you die?" Dwayne was never around anymore to help her shut it up. This had been fine when she was working the same crazy hours as he. Now she had plenty of time to brood over a marriage with an absentee husband and no kids.

The sound of a key turning in the keyhole shook Nonso from her reverie. It was now 2:30 a.m. and there was Dwayne, silhouetted in the doorway. Nonso shaded her eyes when he turned on the lights. "Welcome home," she said.

"What's wrong? Did something happen?" Dwayne had

puffy bags under both eyes from too little sleep. He looked ten years older than he was—his face gray-tinged from exhaustion and a semipermanent furrow of concern on his forehead.

"I had a hard time falling asleep, so I thought I'd stay up and maybe actually see my husband for the first time this week." She'd meant for her tone to be light, easy, but realized she sounded a little angry.

Dwayne winced. "One of the Hong Kong clients is being a total pain in the ass. I seem to be the only person he gets along with. We made major progress with the contract tonight, though; it looks like we'll get this over and done with soon."

"There's nothing worse than a difficult client," she said. An argument at 2:30 a.m. was the last thing they needed.

"Tell me about it," Dwayne said as he shrugged off his suit jacket and tugged at the light blue silk tie she'd bought him a year earlier just because.

"Dwayne, I need a vacation," Nonso blurted abruptly, before he could launch into a monologue about the problems with the client in Hong Kong and with contract law in general.

He looked at her, surprised, the furrow returning to his brow. "In two months we can do Paris or maybe Venice." His face lit up. "Or how about Tokyo again? You always said you wanted to go back."

"I'm thinking Nigeria," Nonso said gently. "For about three weeks. I need to see my family, sit around for a bit and do absolutely nothing."

A vein pulsed in Dwayne's forehead. He bit his lower lip for a moment, then nodded. "Okay. Okay. I hear you."

———

Dwayne took two days off work (a Saturday and Sunday) to drive Nonso to an assortment of outlet malls in New Jersey. A week after the shopping was done, he took her to JFK, their car weighed down by two bloated suitcases filled with all the clothes, bags, shoes, cosmetics, cologne, and beeping toys her Nigerian relatives could desire. A small Samsonite carry-on held Nonso's personal effects. Everything else, including the large suitcases, was a gift. After nine years of marriage, Dwayne had stopped asking why they shopped for people Nonso had barely even met.

Their first major argument as a married couple had revolved around this very subject, ending when she accused him of having a selfish, individualistic, and un-African attitude. She recalled the stunned look on his face, the way her heart had slammed painfully against her ribs at the knowledge that she'd caused more hurt than she'd intended. She'd twined her arms around him, whispering, "I'm sorry," hugging him until he relented and hugged her back. They'd made love soundlessly, each caress erasing the memory of sharp words hurled like jagged stones. Back then, they could never stay mad at each other for more than a few hours, their shared laughter filling up the apartment, brightening the walls and pushing them back, making the small space seem much larger.

———

Nonso turned her head away from the praying passengers so no one would see her roll her eyes in exasperation. The prayer continued until the minibus joined the Asaba-Benin express-way, its small space reverberating with amens each time the preacher paused to draw breath. Nonso wondered idly what Muslims and atheists did when they found themselves in her situation. She suspected they went along with the crowd so they wouldn't stand out. She'd made a decision while in her hometown to speak only Igbo when spoken to, because she feared any English words uttered might betray traces of a life in America. Her Igbo was accentless, no American spir-its seized her tongue when she spoke it. Soon, the minibus's impromptu service was over. The driver popped a cassette of Christian Igbo music into the tape deck and cranked up the volume. Several passengers clapped and sang along, their voices sometimes blending harmoniously, at other times dis-cordant. Nonso smirked as she stared out the window—to her, they sounded like a chorus of night-drunk toads.

———

Fifteen minutes after they'd joined the expressway, Nonso saw a crude barrier: a few ruined tires and spindly-looking tree branches obstructing the minibus's path. It was manned by two figures in black uniforms holding automatic rifles. The minibus choir hushed. Nonso clasped her hands, pressing them together until they ached. In the U.S., she'd finally learned to hide her fear of armed men in uniform, and she drew on that practice now.

The minibus driver slowed down, his posture relaxed as he palmed one of the policemen's hands. The naira-note exchange completed, the policeman gave a broad smile, exposing a set of dazzling white, not-quite-villainous teeth. The bus lurched forward and its passengers sighed their relief. By the fourth roadblock, Nonso was half-asleep; the cash exchanges were going smoothly and no one on the bus or outside it was showing any signs of anxiety.

To keep herself awake, Nonso let her mind drift to the two weeks she'd spent in Anioma-Ukwu with her parents. The huge lopsided grin covering her father's face as his eyes took her in when she arrived. The jolt of shock she'd felt inside because he seemed smaller, his shoulders hunched, his hair much grayer than the last time she'd seen him. Her mother, too. It was as though her parents were slowly shrinking, as if their retirement from university life had robbed them of some vital quality. The dreadful thought that they might not be around the next time she visited Nigeria ricocheted around her head, making her feel dizzy momentarily.

When her mother exclaimed as she clasped Nonso in her

arms, "My God, don't people eat in New York these days; why are you so skinny?" Nonso had dissolved into tears, clinging to her mother's frail form as her body shook with sobs.

"Sorry, I don't even know why I'm crying," she hiccupped finally.

Nonso's mother had looked up into her eyes and said with firm conviction, "It will be well. I will be here to see your children. Now stop that noise and come and eat. I made some okra soup for you with pounded yam."

"Prodigal daughter nah wah oh," her father had teased, thumping her back lightly. "Well, it's good to see your face, even once every six years."

Nonso's three older brothers lived in Lagos, Ibadan, and Port Harcourt—she was the only child who'd chosen to settle outside Nigeria.

Her days in Anioma-Ukwu flew by in a haze of good home-cooked food and outings with Dibia in his jalopy. He talked with pride about the schoolchildren he taught, and pointed out the new school building, which he'd painted bright green with the help of his students.

They drove by a four-story mansion that seemed out of place amid the modest bungalows and two-story buildings of her hometown. "Whose house is that?"

Dibia eyed the building, hawked, spat out the window, and then said simply, "Okafor. The thief."

Nonso marveled at how little Dibia had changed over the

years, her body shaking with laughter at his blunt response. He was as unimpressed with material things at thirty-two as he had been when they were children.

The day before she was to head back to Lagos to catch her flight to New York, Nonso felt moody and listless. That night, she had a dream that she and Dwayne lived in Anioma-Ukwu down the street from her parents. Even though they were in Anioma-Ukwu, they still occupied their Brooklyn apartment, with its mahogany furniture and view of Prospect Park. In the dream, they had two beautiful children: a boy that had Dwayne's honey complexion and soft, hazel eyes, and a girl that had Nonso's high cheekbones and full lips. When the beeping of her travel alarm intruded and the dream melted away, she almost cried out loud from disappointment.

————

Nonso's stomach growled, faintly at first and then aggressively. She'd woken up at five a.m. to make it to the bus stop before seven and hadn't eaten because the thought of food at such an early hour made her feel ill.

The young man to her left held out a bunch of bananas. "Aunty, take some."

An arm from behind offered a few golden-brown akara balls wrapped in newspaper. Touched, she thanked the young man and a woman behind her for their gifts of food, taking two bananas and a ball of akara.

Her hunger sated, Nonso stared out the window at the dense green sea of elephant grass colonizing the sides of the road. The grass hissed, swaying in the breeze, waves broken here and there by squat shrubs, fruit-laden pawpaw trees, and six-foot anthills built from the red Delta earth. Fascinated, she counted anthills, dozing off before she hit ten. She was jolted awake only when the driver pulled the minibus into a motor park dotted with wooden kiosks. The passengers got out to stretch their legs, use the bathroom, and buy food. A plump woman who was sitting behind Nonso (the source of the akara balls) thrust her baby into Nonso's hands—she needed to "ease" herself, she said, and would Nonso watch the child? She was off before a response had even formed in Nonso's brain. She smiled at the baby girl, a round ball with an even rounder head, plump arms and legs. She was clothed in a pink-and-yellow cotton dress, her soft curly hair brushed back and held with one pink and one yellow barrette on each side of her head. Nonso was struck by how much the girl looked like pictures of herself when she was a baby. She tickled the baby's chin and was rewarded with a gurgle and a baring of healthy pink gums. The baby grabbed Nonso's finger and wouldn't let go.

"Baby girl, you've got a fierce grip," Nonso whispered.

The baby giggled in response. Nonso grinned back, but her grin disappeared quickly. It occurred to her that if she and Dwayne had had a baby soon after they got married, their child would be nine years old. A sadness she had kept suppressed for so long washed over her. Suddenly, a thought flashed through her mind. *What if I just keep walking until I find a taxi that will take us to Lagos?* She looked around, her heart thumping wildly. No one was looking in their direction and the baby's mother was nowhere to be seen. A sharp voice shot back. *No, you can't do that. Her mother's face would haunt you for the rest of your life. What is wrong with you? Besides, what do you think this crowd would do to a baby thief, if you were caught?* Nonso shuddered and bowed her head briefly. The baby giggled again, jamming a fistful of dress into her mouth.

"Yeah, let's get some food," Nonso said out loud, her heart-beat not quite back to normal.

With the baby perched on her left hip, Nonso walked toward the scent of moin-moin cooking. The aroma was coming from a brightly painted buka with wooden benches and tables and a few off-white plastic chairs facing its thin, electric-blue walls. She wasn't really hungry anymore, but as she thought of moin-moin cooked in leaves, she remembered watching her grandmother peel and grind soaked brown beans as a child. Nonso always got a bit of shrimp or hard-boiled-egg stuffing for helping to pour the ground-bean mixture into carefully arranged leaves. Unfortunately, it seemed like nobody cooked moin-moin the old way anymore. She bought a cellophane-wrapped pink-orange blob from the buka, shifting the baby from her right hip to her left to free her right hand, and then plunked herself down on a wooden bench, moving the baby to her lap as she sat and ate. After she was done eating, she noticed that the woman with the nine-year-old boy was trying to get him to sit down at a large wooden table, but he was flailing his arms angrily and refusing to listen. Nonso wondered again why he seemed so full of rage.

Swinging the baby back on her hip, she walked over to the boy and placed a hand on his shoulder, saying loudly, "There's a chair behind you."

The woman smiled her appreciation at Nonso, who took the boy's hand and placed it on the chair back, and he eased into it. She sat down at the same table with the baby on her lap, facing him.

"Who is speaking?" he asked.

"It's me," Nonso replied.

He mumbled something—it could have been thanks but she didn't think so. As the woman walked to the buka to place an order, Nonso asked the boy in a fierce, low voice, "Why do you speak to your mother that way? It's so rude, not nice at all."

The boy was silent for a while. "She's my grandmother, not my mother. My mother is gone." He paused. "Mama said if I prayed every day God would spare my eyes and I did every day, every day. She lied to me!"

Nonso didn't know what to say to this. "What's your name?"

"Ike," the boy said.

The baby made a sound, then attempted to jam her tiny left fist into her much smaller mouth.

"Who's that?" Ike asked.

"A baby. She's very pretty and fat, about ten months old. I think she's trying to talk."

The baby started to cry. Nonso jiggled her up and down, singing: "Onye mulu nwa ne b'akwa? Wete uziza, wete uda . . ."

Apparently, the baby had heard this before; she stopped mid-sob with a surprised look. A sweet smile dimpled her cheeks.

Ike asked, "Can I carry her?"

"Yes, of course."

Nonso placed the baby carefully onto his lap, guiding his left hand to support the baby's back. As he passed his right hand slowly over the baby's face, she grabbed on to one of his fingers and gurgled. "She is strong oh," he said, smiling.

———

Nonso spied the baby's mother walking toward them. "Her mother is coming back. Let me have her."

"I think she's hungry," she said to the baby's mother as she handed her back.

"No, I just breast-fed her before we stopped here. Thank you." The woman walked off with the baby, who didn't spare Nonso or Ike a parting glance. Nonso felt just a tiny bit hurt.

Ike's grandmother returned with two plates full of rice and stew, each topped with a tiny lump of meat.

She smiled shyly at Nonso. "Come chop," she said, pushing her steaming plate in Nonso's direction.

"Thank you, ma, I'm okay." Nonso shook her head from side to side and patted her belly.

"So, what is London like?" Ike's grandmother asked, after carefully chewing a mouthful of rice.

Nonso flinched. Even though she'd taken great care to speak only in Igbo, for some reason, people insisted on replying to her in English or pidgin. Now this. "I don't live in London," she said. "Why do you think I do?"

The woman looked at her as if this was a silly question. "Your skin."

Nonso looked down at her arm, then at the woman's and the boy's. They were about the same shade of brown. "What about my skin?" she asked.

"It's so shiny-shiny," Ike's grandmother said.

Shiny-shiny? Nonso thought to herself. *So much for speaking Igbo so you don't stand out.* Suddenly she missed Dwayne, wished he were sitting right there beside her. He had an incredible talent for mimicry; she could almost picture him giving hilarious impressions of the driver, minibus passengers, and motor park vendors. She imagined both of them living in Nigeria, preferably Ibadan, maybe Lagos, in a house like the one she grew up in, with a red ixora hedge surrounding a big yard dotted with

banana and plantain groves as well as mango, pawpaw, and co-
conut trees. She'd grow fluted pumpkins at the back of the
house and use their leaves in soups and yam pottage. They'd
rarely have to buy fruits or vegetables! They could visit her
parents every few months to take a break from the city and
enjoy the tranquility of small-town life. Maybe, *maybe*, they
might even reconsider their original stance on adoption. She
sighed, shaking her head. Dwayne would never go for it.

———

Before she'd quit her investment-banking job, the desire for
a child was like the dull throbbing of a stubbed toe, easy for
her to ignore. And she'd reconciled herself to life without one.
Now it felt like fingers caught in a slammed door.

Sixteen years. They'd been together almost her entire
time in the U.S. They met in a comparative literature class her
sophomore year in college. Dwayne was late for the class. The
door creaked when he opened it and everyone turned to stare.
She'd sucked in her breath at the sight of him: long and lean,
with eyes like butterscotch. When those eyes brushed past all
the others and settled on her face, she'd had the presence of
mind to smile. He sat next to her and she knocked over her
notebook in confusion.

He bent over, picked it up, grinned. "Maybe I should hold
on to this for you?"

A strangled squeak escaped her lips. Then she managed to

regain control of her voice, grin right back at him. "There'll be a price for holding on to it."

By the time midterms rolled around, she was reconsidering her plans to return to Nigeria after graduation if it meant leaving him behind. Dwayne Cuffe was her first and only serious boyfriend.

———

Half an hour after they'd pulled into the motor park, the minibus lurched back onto the Benin-Lagos Expressway, its occupants mostly full and in good spirits. Twenty minutes later, the sky turned a dark shade of gray and angry jets of water pelted the roof. Cries of "Driver slow down, easy oh!" echoed throughout the minibus. Nonso raised the window on her right side as the driver slowed to a crawl through the curtain of water. A Mercedes truck barreled past, going at least 100 miles per hour, the gust of wind it created rocking the minibus slightly.

"Idiot," one alarmed passenger yelled. "Ah ah, you can't even see anything properly in this rain."

"All these crazy drivers," said the woman behind her.

With the rain coming down in silver sheets, all the checkpoints they passed were abandoned; the policemen manning them had probably left to find shelter. After a while, Nonso noticed that it had stopped raining in front of the bus, the tarmac ahead bone dry except for tracks made by cars and trucks coming from the rainy area. Nonso rolled down the window, twisted her neck to the right, and stuck out her head briefly. It was clear ahead of the minibus, but still raining behind it. The driver picked up the pace to make up for lost time. After a while, Nonso saw dark skid marks veering toward the right edge of the road.

"Ehn, look!" she exclaimed to the young man to her left, pointing a finger. Nestled between two sturdy rubber trees was the Mercedes truck that had shot past them earlier, pulled-up shrubs, a baby palm tree, and weeds lying in its wake. Its driver was sitting, rocking back and forth in the twisted wreck of the truck's cab, his head held between his hands and bowed, as if in prayer.

"Foolish, no be you dey drive like crazeman for rain?" the young man to her left shouted.

"God don punish you," someone yelled from the back of the minibus.

"No be God oh, nah devil," the woman with the baby said quickly.

"What will happen to him?" Nonso asked the young man to her left, worried.

"They all carry mobiles. He will call his oga, and his oga will send someone. They will offload onto another lorry."

"He'll probably lose his job," she whispered, more to herself than to the young man.

The young man shook his head. "If his oga sacks him, his

whole family will go and beg until he gets the job back. Don't worry."

A few months before her trip, the vice president at Nonso's bank had fired one of the assistant managers. She tried to imagine what would have happened if the man had returned, his wife, children, mother, and father in tow, to ask for a second chance at his old job. It was a silly scenario to dream up, really. They wouldn't even make it past the security guards.

The young man sighed, shaking his head again in exasperation. "Yes oh," he said. "That is Nigeria for you."

"That is Naija," Nonso said, but she couldn't stop smiling. It occurred to her then that she hadn't felt numb in many days, in fact, not since she'd arrived in Nigeria.

———

The minibus sped on; they were now in Ogun State, close to Lagos. People started pulling out their mobile phones. Nonso turned hers on to let her brother know she would be arriving in Jibowu within an hour, but her GSM phone wasn't picking up any signal. The other passengers seemed to be yakking away on their phones with no difficulty. Nonso figured she'd wait until they got into Lagos, then try calling again. Her brother was to send his driver to pick her up from the Delta Lines stop in Jibowu; she could sit inside the bus depot until the driver arrived. The minibus made steady progress. They were now in Lagos State. Suddenly the young man to her left broke off his conversation and looked around wildly, alarm spreading over his features.

He announced, "Soldiers and area boys are fighting in Jibowu with guns and machetes. Them don kill two people already."

People started making calls of their own. "It's true oh," a woman shouted. "Driver, I beg make you drop me here."

———

The driver pulled the minibus over to the side of the road and passengers scrambled for the exit. Nonso glanced at her phone. It still wasn't receiving a signal. She'd never lived in Lagos and didn't know where they were or how to get to her brother's place in Victoria Garden City.

Nonso began a conversation in her head, bargaining with fate or whatever was out in the universe watching. I've been stuck for so long trying to figure out what to do with my life, but I think I know now. If I can avoid the fighting in Jibowu, get to VGC safely, I'll contribute a lot more than money wired to relatives. I've always felt this nagging guilt about giving my best work years to a country that doesn't really need me because I'm totally replaceable. But here, here I could do so much, share what I've learned. If I make it to VGC, I'll stay. She shivered, feeling a strange mix of fear and exhilaration at this decision, trying not to think more deeply about what staying might mean for her and Dwayne.

The young man to her left said loudly, "Aunty, excuse me."

Nonso was blocking his path out of the minibus. She moved over to the right, opened the door, and stepped out. As he exited, Nonso grabbed his arm, and asked urgently, "How do I get to Ozumba Mbadiwe?" She took care not to mention her final destination.

He smiled and motioned over a man on a motorbike. "Okada, come." Nonso ran to the back of the minibus and grabbed her now battered-looking Samsonite carry-on. The okada driver tied Nonso's carry-on behind the pillion seat with a thick piece of rope, sat back down, and gestured for her to get on. She hesitated briefly, then sat behind him, wrapping her left arm around his middle. They set off. Nonso held her mobile phone in her right hand. Still no reception. After a half hour of weaving in and out of traffic, they got to Ozumba Mbadiwe Road, which she recognized. She was going to be okay. The rush-hour traffic was bumper-to-bumper and stalled. Street hawkers moved unhurriedly, selling soft drinks and food to the car-bound. A burst of elation filled Nonso as the okada kept moving in spite of the go-slow, squeezing into tight spaces a car couldn't. Even if she'd made it to Jibowu, she and her brother's driver would have been stuck for hours in traffic.

"Thank you, thank you, thank you," she said out loud. The driver nodded, as if he had somehow listened in on her earlier bargaining and understood what was at stake. She glanced down at her mobile phone again. Three bars. She dialed her brother's number carefully with one hand, willing her fingers to be steady and not drop the phone. Her sister-in-law's muffled "hello" sounded in Nonso's ear.

"Chichi? It's Nonso!"

"Welcome. Are you at Jibowu?"

"Soldiers and area boys were breaking each other's heads at Jibowu. I didn't go there oh. I'm on Ozumba on an okada. I'll be home soon."

"You're on a what?"

"On an okada."

Shocked silence. Then, "Nonso, are you all right? Your voice sounds funny. Let me know where you are so the driver can come get you."

"He won't even make it with all this traffic. Don't worry; I'll be there soon. And guess what?"

"What?" Chichi sounded apprehensive.

"I'm moving back home!"

"Does Dwayne know this?" There was no concealing the alarm in Chichi's voice.

"He knew I was Nigerian when he married me," Nonso said. "You like to worry oh. Don't worry. Don't worry at all. Everything will be fine." Nonso clicked off the phone. Her brother and his wife owned a sprawling six-bedroom home in VGC. She knew they wouldn't mind her staying with them until she could get her own place.

To stave off a prickle of doubt forming in her belly, Nonso forced her mouth into a wide grin. What would Dwayne think if he could see her now, perched on the back of an okada, huge sweat stain spreading out from under each arm, hair from her weave fluttering every which way? The grin gave way to peals of laughter and then sudden sobs that racked her body.

"Madam?" the okada driver inquired, probably wondering what was going on with his fare.

"Nothing oh. Keep going. Just face the road and keep going."

START YOUR SAVINGS
ACCOUNT TODAY

2004

REMI

Remi rubbed her temples as she stared at the ringing phone, willing herself to pick it up. She knew it was her father from the caller ID, imagined him hunched forward on the leather reclining chair she'd got him for his fiftieth birthday, his forehead cut deeply with worry lines. Her husband, Segun, had taken their seven-year-old twin sons to the park for a pick-up game of futbol. This meant there was no one around to mouth words of encouragement, guide her through the conversation with hand signals and head gestures. Gripping the cheap plastic, she clicked Talk.

"Hello?"

"Hello? Remi? Hello? Can you hear me?" He always started with the same question even when the silence stretching across the Atlantic was static-free.

"Yes, Daddy." She cradled the left side of her face with her free hand.

"How are Segun and the boys?"

She was tempted to pour out all that was bothering her. Daddy, their names are Dele and Akin, not "the boys." Dele wants to be an American football star and bullies his classmates at school. His teacher sent home a note three days ago complaining about his conduct. Dele says he shoved a couple of boys who were making fun of Akin to make them stop. He says I've always told them to look out for each other and that's what he was doing.

I caught Akin wearing my dress, shoes, and makeup last week. He was lip-synching in front of the mirror. He told me he wants to be the lead singer in a girl band. A weird, pulsating pain hit me beneath the ribs and I thought, *The world is going to eat you alive and I don't know how to shield you from it*. So I had him sing for me and I danced along. He laughed and laughed at my clumsy moves and showed me how to do them right but all I could focus on was hiding my fear.

I wake up at night worrying about Segun's health, wondering whether he'll be around to see Dele and Akin go to college. He's already on Adalat for high blood pressure but doesn't remember to take it unless I remind him in the morning. He started graduate school three months ago, after quitting his job. That means money is tight, very tight, right now.

Taking a deep breath, Remi said instead, "Segun and the boys are fine."

"Good, good. We're all fine here as well." Her father cleared his throat. "Emm, Remi, Ola's tuition at the new school has been increased. I wouldn't bring it up, but it gets difficult. Really difficult sometimes."

Ola was Remi's half brother, her father's last child and only son. His main achievement in life thus far was racking up expulsions from school. Twice, it was for fighting other students. Once, he got kicked out for harassing his Yoruba teacher and putting sand in the gas tank of her car after he failed a test. The last expulsion was for spitting at his school's vice principal. He was now enrolled in an expensive military-style boarding school in the northern part of Nigeria.

The clearest memory Remi had of Ola, one that always made her smile, was from his christening. Her father had let her carry the baby up to the church dais; to Remi's surprise, Ola's mother did not object. Remi made faces at Ola while the Reverend Father poured water over his head, sticking her tongue out when he gasped and shuddered from the coolness of the water. She succeeded in turning the shriek of outrage forming on his lips to a fit of giggles. Before the Reverend

Father could hand him over to his mom, Ola hit the water in the cistern with his little palm and it splashed all over the man's robes.

"I think he's baptizing me, too," the Reverend Father said. Everyone in the church laughed, as shafts of sunlight played off glass, illuminating the baby's wide eyes and fat cheeks, his cheerful babble lightening hearts. He'd seemed blessed, destined to be noticed and liked wherever he went. She hadn't seen or spoken to him much since that day and her only insight into his demons was the resentment she felt toward her father. That, she thought, they probably shared: Ola for feeling smothered by his father's attention, her for being deprived of it.

She looked around the living room of the Nanuet, New York, town home she and Segun had bought from an elderly West Indian couple, trying to build up the nerve to say to her dad what she never had before. Dele's and Akin's stuffed animals, dolls, trucks, puzzles, and books were strewn about the room. They covered the worn leather couch and armchairs, camouflaged the discolored yellow patches on the faded turquoise shag carpet that must have served as a beautiful reminder of the Caribbean Sea for the original owners. They'd had the carpet steam-cleaned before moving in, hoping one day to save enough for a renovation. Hardwood floors, maybe. That day had not yet come. The only space free of toys was the dining area with its Thai rubberwood table and matching chairs. She sat now in one of these dining chairs, its dark brown stain marred by cream gashes where the student movers had allowed the exposed wood to get chipped.

"Are you still there?" Remi's father was waiting for a response to his mention of Ola's tuition increase. He let loose a phlegmy cough that startled her.

"Yes, Daddy. Did you start smoking again?" Remi pinched the inside of her right arm with her free hand, hoping the pain would sharpen her resolve.

"It does get very difficult," he repeated.

Her father was the first of three sons born to an aso-oke weaver. When Remi's grandfather married a second wife, her grandmother packed up her boys, returning to a tiny, airless room in her father's home. She couldn't read or write and didn't make much money but decreed that her sons would be college graduates. To make this happen, Remi's father went to work, delaying his education so that he could pay his younger brothers' tuition. As a child, listening to her uncles tell the story of how they graduated with her father's help, she'd felt so proud. Now she was about to break with that example. Remi breathed in deeply. When she exhaled, the words tripped off her tongue. "Don't worry, Daddy, I'll take care of Ola's tuition. How is Mama Ola?"

"Oh, she's fine, just fine. Her shop is doing well."

Remi almost yelled, *If her shop is doing so well, why can't she put up some of the money toward her son's tuition?* but caught herself in time.

"It's good to hear that," she said.

"My card is running out so let me ring off now. Email me when you send the wire transfer to my bank." He hung up the phone.

Up until a year before, Remi would have had him hang up and called him back after she picked up the phone, to save him the cost of the call. Not offering was her most visible sign of protest. Her father didn't seem to notice.

A sour taste bubbled into Remi's mouth and she closed her eyes briefly to steady her thoughts. She was disturbed by the rage that flooded her when she thought of her father's wife. The first time she visited her father's new family, Mama Ola fixed one lazy eye on Remi's face, announcing resentfully as the other eye traveled heavenward, "You're the spitting image of your mother. Let's hope you didn't inherit her character."

"Everyone says she's beautiful. And at least she doesn't have the character of a cross-eyed witch," Remi had said.

Mama Ola opened her mouth to reply but apparently thought better of it, fat tears sliding down her cheeks as Remi's father walked in. The next day, Remi was on her way back to her mom's.

———

Mathematics was the language Remi felt most comfortable with, its clarity and precision a refreshing departure from human speech, which had a way of twisting around to strike where it hurt, when she least expected it.

Like the time when she was eight years old and her mother had said to her: "Won't it be fun to visit your aunt and uncle in Jos and see your cousins?"

Remi had just spent two weeks in the hospital recovering from a gash to her left leg that had required many stitches. She'd come home from the hospital to find her parents moody and not speaking to each other, although they both showered attention on her.

Even when they all sat in the same room, her mother would say, "Tell your father we need money for food."

He'd respond, "Tell your mother she earns a salary too."

She'd never heard them fight like this before; the cold silences frightened her more than anything else. Remi consulted the tiny Cooperative Bank for Africa calendar in her room; her mother's boss had given it to her when Remi spent one of her school holidays at her mother's office. Every morning, she marked off the days left until the trip to her aunt's in Jos and sang the jingle "Wise men bank with CBA, and women too with CBA. Start a savings account today with CBA, CBA." She'd repeat the jingle over and over in a high-pitched voice till her mother said "Oti to! That's enough. Don't kill us with your screeching. I will throw that thing away oh!"

Remi left the bleak parental stand-off in Lagos for the warm cohesion of her aunt and uncle's family in Jos, returning weeks later to a new home in Ibadan that held no sign of her father. There had been no warning that her visit with her aunt, uncle, and cousins would mark the end of her parents' marriage and the beginning of an unsought adventure. One and a half years after the trip to Jos, her mother married a widower with three children. The youngest was ten years older than Remi, and already in university. During the church service, the preacher droned on about the beauty of holy matrimony. Remi rolled her eyes and passed the time counting the days since she'd last seen her father.

As the confetti fell at the end of the ceremony, she yelled, "Three hundred and twenty-two!"

No one paid any attention to what she'd said.

————

Right after the divorce, Remi's mother fell into one super-long bad mood, snapping at her no matter what she did. Remi kept her spirits up by climbing into a tree behind their new house and running through the times tables from 2 to 10. As soon as she got tired of that, she thought about her dad, sure he'd soon come to rescue her, and angry that she hadn't been given the option of staying with him. When they'd lived in Lagos, once every few days he'd show up at her primary school to take her home instead of her mom.

"What did you learn in school today?" he'd ask, and he'd laugh out loud, head tilted back and body shaking as she mimicked her teacher.

"Shuldren, today we must learn our times tables . . . Tree times one tree, tree times two sis, tree times tree nine, tree times four twelf . . . Remi, your stomach is paining you? Ginger Alay is good for stomachache."

It often looked like all 10 million Lagosians were on the roads as they inched their way home in his Toyota Crown, but for Remi, the slow traffic meant more time with her dad. She'd stare longingly at the sweating bottles of Fanta, Coke, and Schweppes bitter-lemon borne by street hawkers weaving through the stalled traffic. He'd buy Remi oranges instead, the rinds taken off with swift strokes of a razor blade, leaving behind geometrical patterns of orange and white. She'd tear off the small cap at one end of the orange and sink her teeth into the fruit's center, spitting pips out the rolled-down car window as she sucked it dry. When she was done, the limp carcass of pulp and outer skin followed the pips out the window. Her mother would definitely have yelled at her for this but her dad let her be.

Sometimes he'd bring her favorite delicacy, suya, newspaper-wrapped and hot from the grill. Her eyes and nose would stream as she wolfed down tender bits of marinated beef and raw onions. He'd buy iced water to soothe her inflamed lips and tongue when she was done licking little bits of suya spice off the newspaper. Then, to distract her from the traffic nightmare, he'd pop an eight-track cartridge into the car's audio system and they'd sing at the top of their voices to Fela Kuti's "Shuffering and Shmiling," which he kept in the car for occasions such as these.

She'd bop up and down in her seat to the beat of the music, rivulets of sweat plastering her orange checked uniform to her back. She'd have given anything to return to those simpler days: singing at the top of her voice, her father tapping the steering wheel in time to the Afrobeat music, the din of blaring horns and a stream of inventive Yoruba curses coming from the irate and trapped drivers surrounding them.

After her mother remarried, Remi saw her father exactly seven times: at his second wedding, during her disastrous visit with his new family, at her half brother's christening, at the airport the day she left for America, at her graduation from college, at her wedding, and on a trip to Nigeria to show him his first grandchildren, when the twins were barely a year old.

She'd majored in mathematics at Rutgers, her favorite subject applied abstract algebra. She soaked up formulas on groups, rings, fields, and lattices. Cryptography fascinated her; the power to create something and hide it forever from those you don't trust, to render a secret unbreakable but hand over its key to the specially chosen. She once tried to explain this to her father but he just grunted and changed the topic. Segun, on the other hand, encouraged her exploration of symbols, lemmas, and proofs. After getting her master's, she landed a job crunching numbers and analyzing risk for a financial services company focused on retirement planning.

———

The weekend before her father called, Remi and Segun left their home early to spend the morning and afternoon with Mrs. Jolayemi, Segun's mom, in Yonkers. She was going to babysit for them so that they could visit with friends in Jersey City on Saturday evening. Remi was looking forward to their time together without the kids; there hadn't been much of that since Segun quit his job and became a full-time graduate student.

Even though Remi supported Segun's decision to leave a dead-end position, she couldn't help feeling occasional flashes of resentment about the whole situation. After his former boss, Tom, the one person who liked his ideas and was a fierce advocate for him, left the U.S. and returned to Australia, Segun stopped getting promoted and things went back to the way they'd been at work: he'd be at a strategy meeting, suggest something, and be ignored. Five or ten minutes later, someone else would propose the same concept and be lauded for it. At first, Segun agonized about it: if he'd worded his idea differently, framed it in just the right way, everyone would have understood. Tom put a stop to all of that his first week as a new manager by asking a simple question. *Didn't Segun just say that?* Unfortunately, Tom left after three years. Segun stuck it out for two more.

Saturday morning at six a.m., Remi and Segun woke to the sounds of their sons bursting through their bedroom door, pulling carry-on suitcases stuffed with clothes and toys. "We're staying with Mama Yonkas this weekend and she's making moin-moin!" Dressed and showered already, the twins forced Remi and Segun to get ready.

Once they arrived at her little two-bedroom condo on Midland Avenue, Mrs. Jolayemi slapped moin-moin on plates and poured piping hot ogi into cereal bowls for breakfast. They never bothered eating before arriving at her home because they would just have to eat again in order to avoid getting her upset. Remi suspected that Mrs. Jolayemi didn't particularly care for her cooking and wished to spare her son and grandsons as much as possible, but her mother-in-law had never said anything directly that she could point to.

"Can I have more sugar in my ogi, Mommy?" Dele shoved a wedge of moin-moin into his mouth as he asked, smacking his lips with pleasure.

"It's 'may I,' and you have just the right amount of sugar," Remi said. "You don't want to rot your teeth, do you?"

"My ogi tastes just fine," Akin said. "Mama Yonkas makes the best moin-moin!"

"Mommy, how come you never make moin-moin?" Dele asked.

"Because like Akin said, Mama Yonkas makes the best moin-moin, which means I don't need to." Remi reached over and tweaked Dele's nose.

"Mama Badan makes good moin-moin too," Akin said, looking apologetic. He was talking about Remi's mom. Her mother-in-law turned aside to hide a small smile.

Segun was on the sofa flipping through an old album. Dele sucked down his last bit of ogi and ran over to look through it with his dad. "That's Papa Yonkas," he said, "and you and Aunty Riyike when you were small. In I-ba-dan." He pronounced the name of the city carefully.

"Good! Do you remember when we went there?"

"Yes," Akin yelled from the dining table. "We visited Mama Badan and Papa Badan and we went to the botanical gardens."

"That was before Papa Badan died." Dele asked, speaking in a rush, "Daddy, how come all our grandpas are in heaven?"

Remi's face froze in surprise. Her mother-in-law said softly, "Don't be silly, you have your grandpa in Lagos."

Dele's face tightened the way it did when he was convinced he was right about something. "I don't know him," he said simply. "We never saw him."

"You talk to him on the phone all the time," Remi said. She realized as she spoke the words out loud that this wasn't strictly true. Her father usually asked after his grandsons quickly and in passing. He never actually conversed with them or Segun directly. His calls followed a pattern: a chat with Remi about a particular financial difficulty that had just popped up, most often related to her half brother, a mixture of sorrow and pride in his voice as he described Ola's latest exploits. The telling was followed by an expectant pause, after which Remi offered to send money, her offer was accepted, and the call ended.

Akin stared at her, an anxious, pleading look on his face. "Mommy, are you okay? Dele, I told you not to say that. I told you. Stop it, you made Mommy sad."

Dele looked at his father and his lip quivered. He lowered his head, moving away from Segun. Then he scrunched his body into a tight ball at one end of the sofa and closed his eyes like he was sleeping.

"Excuse me, I have to go to the bathroom," Remi said, her eyes filling with tears. Mrs. Jolayemi placed a hand on her shoulder and squeezed it just once, nodding. Remi was quiet the rest of the afternoon. On the drive to Jersey City, she told Segun how fed up she was about the state of her relationship with her father. He nodded but said nothing; he'd heard this many times before. Then Remi told him what she was going to do the next time her father called. Segun smiled and shook his head.

"You don't think I can." Remi turned to him, her body tense.

"I don't think you have to," Segun said softly. "But if you want to, do it."

———

Segun and the boys were still out. Remi sat staring at the cordless phone, a wild thing beating in her chest as she remembered a day when she was twelve and upset because her father had canceled a visit. As she sulked, her mother yelled out, "Keep moping because you want to see your father. All he has done is pay your school fees. Anybody can pay school fees. You better thank your stepfather for the clothes on your back, the food you eat, and the fact that you have a roof over your head. Thank him well oh!"

Not long after her parents' divorce, it occurred to Remi that there was something she must have done to upset her father. She traced it back to the time she returned from the hospital with her stitched leg, before her trip to Jos. Those eggshell-fragile days when the air was hot and stifling, and the hostile silence between her parents made her skin itch. One night in particular, something woke her up. The moonlight through her window was bright enough that she could see the yellow and purple patterns on her aso-oke bedspread, the bottom half of an old outfit that her mother had tried to discard and Remi had salvaged. A muffled sound repeated, the sound that had woken her up. Remi made out a figure—her father seated at the end of her bed, his head buried deep in his hands. He was sobbing, quietly but clearly. An ice-cold chill went through her. She couldn't have moved if she'd tried. She shut her eyes tight and willed the image of her weeping father away; it wasn't something she wanted to see then or ever. At some point, she must have fallen back asleep, because when she opened her eyes again, there was sunlight streaming in through the window and her father was gone. She greeted him cheerfully that morning like nothing had happened and he smiled back at her easily, still carefully ignoring her mother.

Years later, she wondered whether she should have said something or hugged him, whether he'd noticed that she was awake and held her shut-eyed silence against her. She tried to make up for it, studied hard in secondary school, winning prizes in physics, math, chemistry, and technical drawing. Hearing her name called out so many times on prize day would make him happy. She was sure of it. He would finally come to visit the boarding school. She wrote her father a letter. But when the day came, the only family members cheering her on were her mother and stepfather. She'd walked up to the podium four times, deaf to the applause, her whole body numb. His reply was tucked into her pinafore pocket. He wouldn't be able to make it, he said, because of a business trip, but he was very proud of her.

———

Remi stared across the dining table at the low cabinet where she stored their good crockery. The cabinet top was covered in a white lace fabric on which sat a dozen framed photos. There was the one of her and Segun on their wedding day, her white dress loose because she'd lost weight from the stress of organizing things, hair braided and swept up in a bun, hands gripping the bouquet of pink roses, peonies, and bougainvillea, the smile on her face radiant. Segun stood tall, striking in a navy-blue tuxedo, his right hand gripping her waist, face all dimples, teeth, and elation. She'd said to him right after that shot, "We're going to take on this world and win, you hear me?" and he lifted her up and twirled her around. "Yes!" She scanned the other photos from left to right. There were five pictures of Dele and Akin at different ages, each year marked by eruptions of new teeth; two of the boys with Segun's mother; one of the boys with Segun and his sister; two of the boys with her mother and their step-grandfather; and one with Dele, Akin, Remi, and her father. Segun had taken that last picture, so he wasn't in it. Remi remembered how carefully she'd dressed the twins that day, how proud she'd thought her father would be of her, how ecstatic he'd be to meet his first grandchildren; no, his first grandsons. The thought that had seeped to the surface, one she had formed after years of observing his unwavering attention and devotion to his only son, even as he seemed to take her for granted: *He may not have much use for me because I'm a girl but they are boys and he will love them.* She could not have been more wrong. They were still hers. In the picture, her father sat stiff and unsmiling next to her on a worn olive-green sofa in his Lagos living room. Remi had a too-wide smile that contorted her face, making her look more terrified than happy. Dele was trying to squirm out of her grasp and reach for Akin, who was frozen mid-wail on his grandfather's lap as he strained to escape into his brother's embrace. She scrutinized that last photo, as if truly seeing it for the first time, a slow flush of anger washing over her.

She lifted up the framed photo and walked into the kitchen, pressing her foot on the garbage can pedal and watching the lid rise, then stopped herself. She ran upstairs instead, to the bedroom that she shared with Segun, and paused before a heavy chest of drawers. She opened the bottom drawer, the one that hid all the clothes she should but couldn't bring herself to throw away: winter long johns that she no longer used but held on to because they were made of silk, scarves with garish patterns—Christmas gifts from colleagues at work, blouses that Segun had bought her before he finally learned that his taste in clothes for her did not match her taste in clothes for herself. She stuffed the frame picture-side down beneath the jumble of clothes, kicked the drawer hard to shut it, and howled, hopping from the pain and growing even angrier. Her foot throbbing, she ran back downstairs to the dining area.

She was trembling as she reached for the phone, dialed her father's Lagos number.

He picked up on the second ring. "Hello?"

"Hello, Daddy, I have to say something." Her voice almost cracked. She walked into the kitchen and braced one arm on the counter.

"What's the matter?"

"Segun is a full-time student. He's not working right now. I can't wire the money. I have to think about my sons. I have to take care of my family. I can't wire it. I can't."

There was a brief silence. Then, "But why didn't you say so when I called earlier?"

Her father's voice was soft now and warm with concern, which riled Remi up even more. "Because I know you're not interested in what's happening here when you're worried about things at home."

"What?" He sounded taken aback.

His confusion angered her even more. "You know, the other day, Dele asked me why all his grandpas are dead. And I told him he was being silly, he had his grandpa in Lagos, and he says, 'I don't know him, we never met him' and . . ."

Her father broke in, sounding deceptively gentle. "Remi, calm down. I ask after them all the time and they saw me when you brought them to visit . . ."

"Six years ago when they were one. They were too young to remember!"

"I really don't like your tone," her father said. "We are not age mates. Why are you shouting?"

"Why am I shouting? Why? Let's see, there's a man who never showed up for visiting day at Fiditi. Who wasn't there on prize day when I won four prizes. Who didn't even know one of my closest friends died after the riot. Who has no clue what life is like in America, how hard it is, how it grinds you down. And that man happens to be my father." She was shaking hard now, almost delirious with fury.

"You will not talk to me like that." His voice was a low rumble, its forced calmness a warning. "You had a second father. He showed up visiting day and prize day and every other day you mentioned. I knew he would be there and I didn't want to get in the way of your new family but I was always focused on the bigger picture—making sure you had a solid education that would guarantee your success no matter what. You think it was easy paying part of the tuition for Rutgers from here? Do you have any idea how much Mama Ola and I sacrificed? You think you are the only one who has suffered?"

Of course, she thought to herself, that's the way he would see things. Heroic, noble sacrifice on his part, ungrateful whining on hers. How else could he live with himself? She took in a deep breath, held it, then expelled it slowly. "I appreciate your paying for my schooling. I do. But there are other things that are also important. I shouldn't have to wonder whether you would have been there more often"—her voice cracked a little—"whether you would have let me stay with you in Lagos if I were a son and not a daughter." It was out now, the question that nagged at her, made her numb with sadness and fear.

She did not expect the harsh laughter echoing across the Atlantic. "You think I would have paid school fees in American dollars if I thought that way? What did they teach you in all these schools? So much for critical-thinking skills." He paused now and let out an agitated, barking cough. When he spoke again, his tone was defensive. "Look, your mother and I didn't see eye to eye on many things, so it was much better that we not be in the same place at the same time. I knew you were fine; there was no plot to ignore you. Remi, I have to go now— I'll need my brothers' help with Ola's situation."

He hung up the phone before she could interject. She knew he wouldn't be calling back. She decided that she would not dial his Lagos number again. His deflection and denial made certain things crystal clear. Remi began to tremble, her body shaking so hard the phone fell out of her hand and hit the floor, the battery flying out of its compartment. She didn't try to pick it up. Wrapping her arms around her body, she leaned against the lone kitchen wall. To calm herself down, she stood and walked up the stairs to her sons' shared room. On the left side of the room, Dele's bed was a chaotic jumble of sheets, bedcovers, toys, crumb-filled paper napkins, and books. She sighed, shaking her head. Her boarding-school-inspired lessons to the twins on how to make their beds each morning had been wasted on him. Akin's bed on the right was neatly made, his teddy bears, Layi and Duro, set down on decorative pillows as if they were taking a nap. Layi was the older teddy bear, deep brown and worn with a missing right eye. Akin would not part with him, even when Duro showed up one Christmas as a replacement. He said that Layi was Duro's father and needed to be around to play with his son. Remi sat down on Akin's bed, grabbing Layi by a plush arm.

"Baba Duro," she said. "My God! I hope tomorrow is a better day." She curled up on Akin's bed, hugging the trusty teddy bear to her chest, and closed her eyes.

AREA BOY RESCUE

2006
BLESSING

I like my madam but sometimes she behave like somebody whose head is not correct. Like yesterday when we were all inside moto. Sunday, the driver, was taking madam to work at that big bank where she be oga.

Sunday and madam were going to drop me at the market on the way to madam's office in Marina. Madam just give me two thousand naira for the onion, pepper, shaki, edo, and cray-fish for soup when we hear *gbaaam skreee* on the right side of the moto. The moto shake *gbiriri*. One big lorry was speeding past us *vroom*. Madam roll down window, look at the side of the moto. She shout, "Mo gbe, that lorry driver has taken the right side mirror. Sunday, follow him."

Sunday try but the traffic for Ozumba that day, no be joke oh. The traffic slow like tortoise wey eat six bowls of fufu, so we no move far at all. Madam look me, say, "Blessing, come." She jump out the moto, call okada. Me and her, we jump on the back of the motorcycle and she tell the okada driver, "Follow that lorry."

I start to sing in my head, *tantananana tan tan tantananana tan tan*, like that movie I like, the first movie I see when I leave village, reach my sister house for Lagos. Oh—wetin be the name of that movie again? You know the actor. Jamesu. Jamesu Bondu. My madam think say she be Jamesu Bondu.

————

Harmattan season just start when I begin housegirl work for madam last year. Sunday tell me say madam Nonso na big woman. When she say, "Just get it done, I don't have time for your silly excuses," all the worker for bank go say, "Yes, ma, right away, ma, thank you, ma!"

I look Sunday after he tell me the story. "Sunday. Sunday. Sunday!!! How many times I call you? You think I just come from village yesterday? I don live Lagos three years oh. You and this your fabu." You see, madam look very young, younger than my older sister.

Sunday say, "I swear. I swear. God punish my nyash if I dey lie. I see am with my own two korokoro eyes. Blessing, my advice to you oh, no vex madam, she no dey joke if you vex am. Her eyes go red like pepper when she vex. She no dey joke at all."

————

That lorry driver wey jam our moto, he no know which kind woman dey for inside. Me and madam, we follow the lorry, the okada driver know how to speed oh. When the lorry stop for light, the okada stop for lorry driver side. My madam shout, "You took off my side mirror, you idiot." The light change and the lorry driver just speed off like say he no hear the thing wey madam talk. Madam come vex well, well. She say, "Okada, follow that man, I will show him pepper, today is today!"

We follow lorry for Ozumba, lorry turn for Apongbon Bridge, we follow am. Small time, I hear moto horn, *pampam-pam*. When I look, Sunday dey behind us for inside moto. Sunday overtake the okada, overtake the lorry, use the moto block the road, so the lorry no fit pass. I tell you, na real Jamesu Bondu today.

The high-heel shoe my madam wear yesterday na the kind Yoruba people dey call kikelomo. Everytime she wear that shoe, when she come back from work, she go say, "Blessing, bring my slippers, a rag, and the box."

Then I go enter her room bring the box. E get one writing for the side of the box, the writing say: S-a-l-v-a-t-o-r-e F-e-r-r-a-g-a-m-o. I fit spell am, I no fit say am, but that na the name of the shoe. That shoe na the only one wey madam dey keep for box. Real kikelomo, special. Today oh, she no care.

She come take the kikelomo shoe climb lorry side, slap the lorry driver, *tawai*. "Are you crazy? You swipe my car and just drive off, you must be mad. Ori e o da!"

The driver say, "Ehn, you slap me? You this woman, you slap me? Take time oh. Take time. I have your type at home."

Foolish man. I'm sure him wife no fine reach my madam dog. How he go get wife like my madam for home? I hiss, loud.

Madam say, "E ma gba mi l'owo ode yi! You have whose type at home? When I finish with you today, you will know which type you have and which type you don't have. Oya, bring your particulars and insurance, your company is going to repair my car." She hold the lorry driver shirt.

He say, "You this woman, leave my shirt oh, and tell your driver to comot car for road. My company no go pay you nothing. See the nonsense car wey you dey drive. Nah for common Honda you dey make noise so? If to say na Mercedes I spoil, ehen, we for begin talk."

Madam say, "Blessing, write down the vehicle number."

I take the shopping list and the pencil for my bag write down the number. Then we hear, "Wetin dey happen?" I turn and fifteen area boy surround us for bridge. I no hear them when they arrive. Yesterday hot like roast yam for fire, but when I hear "wetin dey happen?" my body cold like Pure Water.

I say, "Madam, madam!"

Madam step down from the lorry side say, "This man bashed my car, refused to stop, and has been abusing me anyhow."

One area boy sing, "You don bash my car? Gbese repete!" The area boys open lorry door, drag the driver, begin dey beat am. "You think you can talk to a woman anyhow like that? Nonsense!"

When the area boys beat am, I come see blood for the lorry driver face, I almost faint. Madam kneel down for ground say, "Na God, I take beg you, please stop beating him. Please stop beating him, don't kill him."

"Ah, no oh," say one of the area boys, "he will learn lesson today. How to treat woman properly."

Madam say, "Please, na God, I take beg una. E do."

The area boys tell the lorry driver, "Say you are sorry."

The lorry driver say very quiet, "I'm very sorry, madam, it will never happen again."

Two area boys begin kick the lorry driver. "Is that how you say sorry? Useless man."

Madam say, "Please, please stop. I accept his sorry."

One area boy say, "Okay. Madam pay us money and we go leave am."

Madam open her bag, take all the money wey dey inside give the area boys. Them count the money begin dey smile. "Thank you, madam. You see, foolish man, madam has saved you. Drive better next time." Na so the area boys leave.

The lorry driver lie down for ground, hold him head for hand. He say, "Yeh, yeh, yeh, my head oh." Blood dey for him face.

Madam say, "Are you okay?"

The driver say, "Yes, ma," stand up, get inside lorry.

Madam say, "Blessing, come let's go home."

The okada driver say, "Pay me my money oh." All this time he just dey look like Lukman.

Since madam no get any money again, I take the money for soup give the okada man. Me and Sunday and madam come enter moto.

Madam say, "Drive back to VGC. I'm not going to work today." She take GSM call the people for office. "I was in a fender bender, I'm not feeling well. I'll be in tomorrow." I like the way madam dey blow grammar sometimes. Fender bender.

When we enter gate, we see Uncle Emeka driver and him Mercedes for there. Uncle Emeka na madam older brother. One tall, yellow man comot for the back of the Mercedes.

Madam scream, "Dwayne," hold the man like say she just comot for prison after thirty years, see her papa. "Dwayne, I'm going crazy in this place, I can't live here anymore. I just slapped a man because he took off my side mirror. Then some area boys appeared and my heart started beating like I was about to have a heart attack. I'm becoming someone I don't like."

"Nonso, slow down, slow down. Shh, shh, shh," oga Dwayne say.

Oga Dwayne na madam husband wey dey for America. The man no be Nigerian, na oyibo. He no fit speak pidgin or Yoruba or Igbo (I ask madam one time). I no know why she marry person wey no fit speak, but the man fine oh, no be small, except him eyes wey get one funny color like that. When madam think say person no see am, she go put oga Dwayne picture for lap, begin cry.

———

That night I wake up because madam dey shout, "Oh! Oh! Oh! Dwayne." I laugh small. I know say oga Dwayne dey chook am. I know because of oga Fapitan. Before I come work for my madam, I get another madam, Mrs. Fapitan. The woman fat like overripe ube, she no get job, and she like to abuse people.

Everyday, "Blessing, you are so lazy. Blessing, haven't you finished cleaning the rooms? It's time to start cooking; oga will be back home soon."

As she dey call my name anyhow, she go sit for sitting room dey watch Channel O, Silverbird TV, or CNN International. She go send me to Tantalizers for meat pie, chicken pie, sausage roll, and Ribena, finish everything for plate, *kom-kom-zam-zam*. She no go give me even small to taste. After I walk one hour for sun to buy am! Me too, I like meat pie and chicken pie and sausage roll. I hate that woman, no be small. Wicked, lazy thing.

One day when she go hairdresser like she dey go every

week, I give oga Fapitan food. He look me, put him hand for my backside, say, "Blessing, Blessing."

I look the man, laugh, say, "Yes, sir?"

Oga Fapitan tall too, but he no tall reach oga Dwayne. As him wife fat, na so him skinny like dogonyaro stick. He play tennis every morning.

After oga Fapitan eat finish, I wash the plates, go boysquarters. Small time pass, then oga Fapitan knock the door for my room, *kom-kom-kom*. I know say na him, because I see the way he look when he say "Blessing, Blessing." Na like goat wey no eat for five days come see big yam tuber. I no surprise—I be fine girl. Him wife no get sense at all. If to say she be good person, I for no answer the man. I unlock the door, say, "Come in."

Oga Fapitan look me, look the old Vono mattress wey dey for floor. He say, "Blessing, see what you are doing to me."

I say, "Sorry, sir, I no know say I dey do you anything."

He laugh, hold me tight. His thing dey hard like pako. He remove my skirt, remove him trouser, say, "Blessing, Blessing."

I say, "Yes sir."

He put me for mattress begin dey chook me. As he dey chook me, the thing sweet me well, well, I begin dey shout, "Oh! Oh! Oh!"

Oga Fapitan say, "Blessing, lower your voice. Everyone will hear you."

But the thing sweet me too well, I no fit lower my voice,

so he take him hand, cover my mouth, so na to him hand only I dey shout, nobody else fit hear. When he finish, oga Fapitan say, "Blessing, did you like that?"

The man deaf? I tell am the truth, "Yes, sir."

Before that day, the only person wey chook me na that small boy I marry for village. My mama say, "No marry am, the boy no get money and you never finish school." But I marry am. He dey form five when I dey form four for secondary school.

After we marry five months, him say he dey go Lagos, he go send for me. One year he no send money, no write letter. I leave my village go for my sister house for Mushin. She say she never see am, that small boy wey I marry.

The next time for boysquarters, oga Fapitan ask me, "Blessing, what do you want to do in life?"

I tell am, "I want to sew the kind clothes women dey wear for *Ovation* and *City People* magazine. The kind all the Lagos Big Girls dey wear."

He say, "Okay." That week, he buy me sewing machine.

One day, when oga Fapitan come see me for boysquarters, him wife bang the door *gbos-gbos-gbos*. She say, "Blessing, I will kill you today." Oga Fapitan wear him trouser, open door, comot. The man no even look my side. The woman come slap me, say, "You think you can steal my husband like that?" so me too I slap am, say, "Na your husband come find me for boysquarters, no be me go find am!" She say make I pack my load now, now, so I pack am go my sister house for Mushin. That Fapitan woman no pay me my money.

———

I find new job at the house of one madam, where my sister husband work as driver. Madam Fapitan call my new madam one day tell am say I dey steal husband. The new madam, she say, "Blessing, you are a very hard worker, but I don't like all this business of people calling my house with stories about you. I know Mrs. Fapitan and this is all so messy. Take this money, I will help you find a new position." The new madam know madam Nonso. Na so I come meet madam Nonso. I tell am the thing wey happen for oga Fapitan house (but I no tell am say the chooking sweet me oh).

She look me, say for Igbo, "I can't believe what those people did to you. Don't worry, there is no man of the house to bother you here. When I'm at work you will go to sewing school."

She give me the job. I tell am say she no go regret am. Na so I begin sewing school.

Madam Nonso show me how to buy share, whether na bank share oh or cement company. She pick the one wey dey pay good dividend for me. She also help me open savings account where I dey put some of my money. The woman, na God send am. I know say she no go last for our obodo country.

One day Mrs. Fapitan call madam Nonso. Na me pick up the phone and she say, "Foolish girl. Let me speak to the madam of the house."

I say, "Hold on," but I want cry because I come see say no matter where I go, this woman go purshue me make them sack me. I no fit drop the phone because madam Nonso dey for sitting room dey look me.

She say, "Who is that?" I say na my former madam. Mrs. Fapitan. I only hear madam Nonso side. She say, "You should be ashamed of yourself. Why don't you face your husband? For god's sake, the girl is less than half his age. You have children older than her!"

Then she begin with the big grammar, something, something, leche and sploiting and she shout at the woman. Me I no understand that part, but I dey laugh inside when she abuse Mrs. Fapitan well, well.

When she put down the phone, I come ask her say, "Sister, wetin be leche and sploiting?"

She say, "Lecherous and exploiting describe a dirty old man."

I say, "But oga Fapitan is not dirty. He bathe every day."

She look me, say, "Blessing, what am I going to do with you?"

Which kind question be that? So I say, "Nothing, ma."

Then she begin laugh ke-ke-ke-ke, so me too I begin laugh. We laugh and laugh and laugh, then she say, "Blessing, you must really learn to sew well, you hear?"

I say, "Madam, I can sew fine skirt now!" I decide say I go sew am something, so I measure her skirt and blouse when I dey wash them.

———

The morning after oga Dwayne come, na Saturday. Normally madam go go work, even on Saturday, but when I go to sweep corridor I hear them dey talk for room.

Madam Nonso say, "I needed some time to get my head together, to think about everything."

Oga Dwayne say, "So why does it feel like I'm being punished? We can do this thing but you have to expand your idea of what it means to have a family."

I go for kitchen, begin cook. Madam Nonso like yam and egg but I think say oga Dwayne no go fit chop am, so I make scramble egg, bread, and tea.

Madam Nonso come for kitchen. I tell am, "Good morning, sister."

She say, "Good morning, Blessing. That smells wonderful!" She look the pots, say, "Oh. You didn't make yam."

I say, "Because oga Dwayne no go fit chop am."

She laugh, say, "He eats yam and jollof and mai-mai and fufu and egusi. The only thing he doesn't like is okra or ogbono soup."

I say, "Chineke! You go teach am Igbo? Dat na the only thing wey remain."

She laugh and laugh. Then she look me, look her foot. She say, "Emm . . . Blessing. I'm going back to America."

That one no surprise me at all. How her husband go dey America and she go dey Nigeria? How them go born pikin? When I see oga Dwayne yesterday, I know say she go go. Na yesterday I begin to think wetin I go do when she go.

Then she say, "I will try to find you another madam."

So I say, "It's okay, ma, I can apprentice and sew. I can sew for you even when you dey America. For your friends, too." I look for ground, scratch my leg. "Una fit pay me dollar when I send you the cloth."

She say, "Ehn?"

I say, "Sister, I dey come."

I go find the woodin up-and-down wey I sew for madam. I take money from inside my savings buy the cloth. For the blouse and skirt, I copy the style from one style she like very much when we look *Ovation* one day. I bring the up-and-down say, "Sister, na for you. Thank you very much."

She say, "Blessing, ehn? You sewed this? It is beautiful!" She hold me, begin dey cry! So me too I cry. I tell you before say madam Nonso dey behave like person wey him head no correct. Today I come see say her head correct. Her head correct pass many people own.

MESSENGER

2050

AISHA

I like the warm texture of silence, the forgotten corners of it, how it can envelop you in its richness, rub softly against your cheeks. Savoring a nice, comfortable silence is one of the joys of my life these days. In the Year of Our Lord 2050, after seventy-eight years on this earth, I've already said most of the things I want to say, and I'm learning so much from what the silence has to tell me.

My granddaughter, Ife, is not of the same mind. Silence for her is a gaping pit to be stuffed with nervous, mindless chatter; it's as though if she stops to draw breath she might fall in and never find her way back out.

"Mamisha," she goes, "can you believe that ThankGod and

I were chosen for the mission this time? I've been praying for this opportunity for a year now."

Ife's school, the Divine Winners University for God's Blessed and Favoured, does regular missions up in the northern part of Nigeria, hoping to win new souls for Christ in the guise of providing impoverished Muslims with aid. There are lots of poor people in her state but they are already Christian and according to their pastor-governor, their poverty stems from not believing enough. ThankGod is Ife's fiancé, a blockhead for Christ, if such a thing is possible. There was a time when I would have put my foot down and said, "No descendant of mine marries a ThankGod, a GoodNews, or a GodReigns," but Yoruba, Igbo, and Hausa names have been out of fashion for the last quarter century, replaced by random English and Arabic phrases from religious texts and pamphlets. My husband, Ade, and I picked Ife's name, Ifeoluwapo, at her parents' request and they acted reasonably happy with the choice. I try to pretend I don't know that Ife calls herself God'sLove when I'm not around. What she and her friends choose to call themselves when they are together is their decision—as long as that phrase is not on her birth certificate and she doesn't use it near me, I'm fine.

———

I had my first child, Okri, at thirty-nine, my second, Iyanu, my miracle girl, at the age of forty-five. Iyanu got married at sixteen, in her first year of university. It took me years to get over the shock. Ade said then that she was probably rebelling against having such old parents. As I sobbed uncontrollably, he gathered me into his arms and rocked me gently. Whispered, "Aisha, Aisha, it'll be okay. She's still working hard at her degree. Iyanu has your fire and my patience. You know that. She'll be fine." She pulled it off, too. Had a daughter at seventeen and graduated with honors at twenty-one. And so here is Ife, my only grandchild, engaged to a moron at sixteen and dressed like a nun from the 1980s, except her habit is royal blue instead of black. At a time when the Catholic Church has agreed that priests can marry and women can be ordained, my granddaughter is asserting her right to be a throwback.

As if that's not enough, now, my son is dying. Okri, my beautiful boy is dying and I can't tell his niece or his sister. Their incessant prayers and caterwauling, their inability to come up with any course of action in an emergency beyond prayers and kneeling before pastors in supplication, *that*, that would literally snap my neck bones in two. *Where did I go wrong? Should we have stayed in America?* I'm trying to keep it together. I need to keep it together.

———

"Mamisha," Ife says again, "isn't that wonderful news?"

I sigh, eye her outfit, and shake my head. "When I was young, my father would drive us to his village up north from

Lagos. I was always frightened by the elehas we passed on the way, covered from head to toe in black in spite of the heat, how I could see nothing but their eyes. I vowed that I would be nothing like those women. And here is my granddaughter, dressed like an eleha."

"Mamisha," she says, a grin on her face, "I bet they didn't look as good as I do. Or wear killer shoes." She points her feet toward me as she speaks and I have to agree that her rhinestone-studded, strappy blue wedges with the six-inch platform heels are definitely chic. And make absolutely no sense with that outfit.

"We used to wear platforms in my day too. Can you girls today do anything original?"

Ife starts giggling helplessly. The girl takes nothing I say seriously.

———

When I was growing up, Nigeria had nineteen states and none of them were strictly defined by religious affiliation. Now we have eighteen Christian states in southern Nigeria, two Christian and two Islamic states in the middle belt, and eighteen Islamic states up north. There was once a forty-first state for people who practiced traditional religions, but the one thing that the self-described "people of the book" from across the country were able to agree on was depopulating that one state. Its land was absorbed by two neighboring states after the last of its residents filed for refugee status and fled to Cameroon. They still live there in camps.

I live in Irawo, the only Catholic state in southern Nigeria. If you had told me in 2015 that I'd be happy living in a Catholic state in 2050, I would have laughed out loud. But here I am, in the most progressive state the Nigerian federation has to offer. My home is in the Irawo Citizens Center, a large complex built by Ade and me and a few of our colleagues who decided to return to Nigeria from the U.S., the U.K., Australia, and Canada. We produce our own electricity with an extensive array of micro solar cells, have our own boreholes and water purification system, grow the food we eat and export what we don't consume. We farm 400 hectares of land using all the advances discovered by the International Institute for Tropical Agriculture and disseminated to and studiously ignored by Nigeria's Ministry of Agriculture.

The center's achievements pretty much mirror those of Irawo State as a whole. This was easy because in spite of being agnostic, Ade was elected to office and served as governor of Irawo for sixteen years. In that time, he was the only state governor who wasn't an imam or a pastor. He recognized that the world was moving to renewable energy because of climate change, that we needed to wean ourselves off of crude oil revenue, take maximum advantage of the sun, and position the state to be a net exporter of power and crops. What he didn't recognize was that these accomplishments by a nonreligious leader might be viewed as a threat by our less-visionary neighbors.

Ade was assassinated five years ago. I spent the first two years after his death in a Valium-induced haze of confusion. On a cool morning, three months after the second anniversary of his assassination, I woke at five a.m. and made a pot of Yirgacheffe, Ade's favorite coffee. I sat, staring at the steam rising from his coffee cup, and let the truth settle into my brain—he would never join me again at our small kitchen table, never clink his coffee mug against mine and grin at me cheekily, "Cheer up, grumpy—it's another sunny morning." Two weeks later, I parceled out most of our belongings to relatives and friends and moved into the room at the Center that now serves as my home.

———

I married Ade two and a half years after divorcing my first husband, Andrew. Ade and I had been friends since law school and continued to be just friends for a year after my divorce until our relationship turned romantic. He'd studied mechanical engineering in college but decided after working for a few years on propulsion systems for a ship builder that he wanted to become an intellectual property lawyer.

Ade was born in Oakland, California, to immigrants who made sure their children spent time with family in Nigeria every summer. I'd visited his folks many times over the years with other groups of friends. His mother liked me well enough when I was just a friend but once it was clear that I might become a daughter-in-law, her attitude changed. She wept the first time she saw me after Ade proposed, telling me her son was a bachelor who deserved a bride that had never been married, who was younger than him, one without a child, asking me to "do the right thing." I did. I married him.

Now here I am with a grandchild who has the best of intentions but is possibly the most gullible creature the universe did ever bring forth. I often find it hard to believe that we're related. Ife is bent on saving me. She believes that I'm going to burn for eternity because I'm not her kind of evangelical Christian, not any type of evangelical Christian. I like to say to her, "My father was Muslim and my mother a nonpracticing Christian. You can keep your heaven if more than half my family will burn. I'd prefer to keep them company." Whenever I say that, she goes quiet, big eyes pooling with liquid as she struggles to come up with a response. She never can, not for those dead and gone already.

Since Ife is my most regular visitor, I've decided to make the most of her company. I tell her stories from way back, try to give her advice, and she listens and laughs but always gets back to the pressing question of my eternal salvation.

I'm getting tired and Ife is still going over the preparations that she and ThankGod will need to make for their mission up north. There's a light that comes into her eyes when she gets on the topic of winning souls, a fierce, fanatical burning that makes me wonder about her sanity. This time, when I see it, I get up and give her a hug. She stops mid-sentence, shocked.

"I have to get ready for my dinner with Nonso and Dwayne," I say.

"It's today?" She looks hopeful. "I haven't seen Mama Nonso or Papa Dwayne in a long time."

When she was younger, Ade and I would take her along to our dinner gatherings, but tonight is special. I have a favor to ask of my friends and I don't want anyone else there when I ask it.

"Maybe next time," I say, then feel a pang of guilt. I hug her again. "Take good care of yourself, and I want to hear all about the mission after you return."

Ife looks positively alarmed (she knows I have absolutely no interest in missions). She opens her mouth to speak. *Mami-sha, are you feeling all right*, I imagine she wants to say, but then she presses her lips together and tries a small smile instead. She's more observant than I'd given her credit for.

———

Okri left me, left Nigeria behind at the age of eighteen to be closer to his father in America and there was nothing I could say or do to stop him. I remember when he was a little boy, he would do anything to make me happy. He hated okra, ugu, spinach, kale, any green veggies, so I told him that it made me very happy when he ate them. He'd stuff the food into his mouth, chewing miserably until he'd cleaned his plate or I let him know that I felt happy enough for him to stop eating. That strategy would never have worked with Iyanu. Okri was such a sweet boy, I guess I wasn't ready for his teenaged self, the moodiness, the thinly veiled contempt, the know-it-all attitude.

Eight months after he turned eighteen, he cleared out his savings account, bought a one-way ticket to the U.S., and asked to speak to me and Ade on an afternoon in late July, once we both got home from work. Seeing the serious look on his face, I sent Iyanu over to the neighbors' house to play with their daughter, who was the same age. Okri made his way to the dining area of the living room and sat at the oval dining table. I deliberately chose a seat directly opposite him and Ade sat to my right.

Okri looked down at his hands but spoke slowly and clearly. "I have to go see to my dad because I'm the only person left in the world who really cares about him."

My face tightened. Always pushing my buttons, this one. Ever since he turned fourteen. "That's not true," I said, determined not to let my voice rise in anger. "We all care but he's in jail, so what can anyone do?"

"I've been admitted to a college in Kansas," he said, staring at Ade, refusing to look at me. "I'll be able to visit Dad weekly."

"Okri, you're supposed to start at UI this autumn. We decided that already. I've visited your father and spoken with him."

"A year ago."

"We don't exactly live next door . . . ," I began. Okri shot me a look that was so hostile that for a minute, I forgot to breathe. My heart began to thump loudly in my ears the way it did when I was about to lose my temper. I jabbed my right index finger in his direction, about to go off, but Ade grabbed it in his left hand and squeezed to get me to calm down.

"That's why I'm moving to Kansas," Okri said, ignoring my distress. "There, I can see him regularly."

"Okri Nowak! If you think I'm going to allow you to throw your life away hanging around some prison, you must be smoking something."

"I'm eighteen. I'm an adult. I've bought my plane ticket and I have a scholarship to go to college in Kansas," he said, speaking slowly and enunciating as if I were hard of hearing. "I'm telling you, not asking for your permission."

I thought about Okri researching colleges in Kansas, contacting them about the application process, scholarships, and financial aid options, arranging to take the SATs, filling out applications and taking tests in secret, mumbling *fine* whenever I asked how he was doing, shrugging when I asked about his friends, what they were up to and why he wasn't joining them, telling myself, *He's just getting older and doesn't want to share everything with his mom like he used to*, asking Ade to speak with him, make sure he was all right. Okri had let me believe that he was okay with going to UI. My eyeballs prickled with tears and my lips began to tingle but I was determined not to show how wounded I felt. I sat for a moment in perfect silence, staring at this stranger with my ears, eyes, and mouth sitting across from me, telling me how little he needed me, how irrelevant I was in the grand scheme of his life. He stared right back at me without blinking, equal parts insolence and bravado.

"Oh, you're a big man now, aren't you?" I so badly wanted to slap the stupid smirk off his face. "Maybe you should find someplace else to sleep tonight since you're all grown . . ."

Ade interrupted. "Aisha, let me speak with you in the kitchen. Okri, stay right there. I need to talk to your mom."

"Yes, Baba." He spoke the words softly, looked at Ade, leaned back in his chair and smiled, all the tension leaving his body. I knew then that I had lost. I wasn't yet sure exactly why but as I got up from the dining table, I understood that nothing would ever be the same again with him and me.

After Ife leaves, I survey my room. It's a nice size, about twenty feet by twenty-four feet, with a recessed walk-in closet. There are three wooden armchairs with plush blue cushions arranged around a coffee table; a mahogany vanity with a mirror and a cushioned stool where I put on my face; a chest of drawers; a small brown leather sofa; and a double bed. The bed has an intricate headboard design; polychromatic wood carved in the style of the late Olowe of Ise. One hundred and fifty years after he was born, a group of Irawo sculptors opened up an art school honoring his style. Their headboards and doors are in demand as far away as Australia. Mine has four panes depicting different scenes: a hunter with his bow and arrow on a quest to catch sleep, I guess; a copter rising into the clouds with a man's head covered by an abeti-aja cap visible through the window of the craft; a palm wine tapper, rope around his middle, halfway up a palm tree; and, my favorite, two mothers with sleeping infants strapped to their backs playing a game of ayo. Just looking at that pane, I can hear the satisfying plop-plop of seeds hitting the wooden board with its scooped-out hollows. My friend Nonso and I used to play ayo in boarding school and the other girls would laugh at us because it was a game only old people played. She had a portable version with a hinge and lock that folded up. Her grandmother, Fodo, gave it to her as a gift and taught Nonso how to play. Nonso taught me and I was hooked.

On my chest of drawers is a lost-wax sculpture of a tall, skinny man and woman entwined in an embrace. Ade bought it during an official trip to Burkina Faso. When he returned, he asked me to close my eyes and stretch out my hands. I loved the weight of it. We were going through a rough patch then, in the first year of his governorship when I hadn't yet acquired the tact that a political wife needs and was being ridiculed constantly in the papers for my "absurd ideas" and the "fact" that I was "bringing [my] husband down."

He said, "We'll always be solid. Just like this. Always."

My heart stopped beating for a minute and then something inside me seemed to break free and I felt lighter. I didn't know how much I needed to hear what he said until he said it. And I stopped reading those stupid newspapers.

In the chest's top drawer is a Chicago Cubs baseball cap (Andrew's favorite team), a one-zloty coin that I saved from my first trip to Poland, and a four-by-six black-and-white photo of my friend Solape, who died while we were in boarding school. She has a teeny-weeny afro and is wearing a gleaming white, freshly starched blouse and carefully ironed skirt, hands on her hips as she smiles for the camera. She always did look sharp. I've carried that photo with me everywhere; it's been to all the states in Nigeria, all over the U.S., to Ghana, Kenya, Zanzibar, Zimbabwe, Botswana, Poland, England, France, Egypt, Brazil, Belize, Mexico, South Africa, New Zealand, Australia, Cambodia, and Thailand. Her dream was to explore space as an astronaut but traveling by plane is the closest thing I can give her. I know that she's sharing this journey with me and I like to think that she isn't too disappointed by the choices I've made along the way.

The other item on my chest of drawers is a clear glass

bottle of water in the shape of a woman in a boubou and gele from the Ikogosi warm springs. Ade, Nonso, Dwayne, and I visited thirty years ago when it was still relatively unknown outside of the southwest and I saved that bottle. Now it's a massive tourist center that sells bottles of water "from Nonso and Dwayne."

On the coffee table is a picture of me, Ade, Okri, and Ife, shot at the top of Table Mountain when we went to Cape Town for a family vacation in 2023. Next to it, there's a framed picture of me and Ade, Remi and Segun, Nonso and Dwayne at a party in Brooklyn, taken before Nonso and Dwayne relocated permanently to Nigeria in 2014.

I make my way to the closet and pick out a pink boubou and a stiff pink-and-purple damask headwrap. Next, I put on a chemise, wear the boubou, and sit at the vanity to tie my headwrap. Makeup is next: I set the foundation, apply dark brown liner to my eyes, fill in my plucked eyebrows. My lipstick is conservative, a deep, dark brown. I stop to admire my handiwork. With my gray hair covered, I could pass for fifty-nine. My hands give me away, though, the veins thick and bulging, fingers gnarled, with deeply ridged nails. My heart beats calmly, steadily. The copter pilot pages me on the intercom.

"I'm on my way," I say.

I pause at the door, run my fingers over its carved wood, and take one last look at the room. Then I turn and walk toward my future.

———

Nonso and Dwayne meet me on the helipad of their mansion; I give him a quick hug and lock her in an embrace that lasts almost a minute as we rock from side to side and coo about how long it's been. Our last dinner gathering was three months ago.

"Aisha, it's so good to see you," says Dwayne when Nonso and I finally break our embrace.

"My personal people! You both look younger every time I see you!" I wink at Dwayne because Nonso gets annoyed when I say that. "What's the secret? Bathing in the tears of Africa's baby leaders?" Since our last dinner, Nonso and Dwayne have been busy visiting their leadership academies across the continent, which are renowned for the breadth and depth of their curricula.

Nonso is unperturbed today. "I brought a glass of our new Malbec up for you. From the vineyard in Jos." She pours me a glass and then we head to the elevator that leads from the helipad into the main house.

I take a sip and smile, warmth spreading in my belly as I realize that I haven't eaten much today and it becomes clear to me how much I've missed my friends. "I'm sure Remi is in the kitchen fussing over an overstirred pot," I say.

Nonso insists on cooking our dinners herself, with occasional help from Remi and me. She dismisses all the staff for the day and we have a simple meal as we share updates from our lives without fear of being overheard or our words misconstrued. We usually sleep over and head back to our respective homes early the next morning after the staff return to prepare breakfast.

In the living area, Segun is sprawled on a sofa watching futbol on TV.

"For the Sege!" I say. "Some things never change."

"Aisha, you have come with your wahala again," he says, chuckling. We hug. "It's good to see you."

"Where is your worse half?" I head to the kitchen and the wonderful aroma of curry, black pepper, and other spices wafting from it. "Remi, hope nothing oh? Are you fighting the pots today or are they fighting you?"

She drops the spoon she was stirring with and squeezes me until I yelp. "How can someone so skinny feel like a boa constrictor? Segun, please come and rescue me from your wife."

We laugh like it's the old days, the weight of what I'm about to share lifting for a moment.

Nonso has made a one-pot dish, with some help from Remi: yam pottage with palm oil, chunks of smoked mackerel, a hint of sweet plantain, and loads of chopped ugu leaves. We fall to, and once everyone is sated, the conversation turns to family and important projects. Since Nonso and Dwayne couldn't have children of their own, they've pretty much "adopted" thousands of kids across Africa and the diaspora and given them a solid high school and university foundation.

They have so many stories about their brilliant protégés; hearing them gives me some hope for the future.

Remi and Segun go on about their twin boys, my godsons: Dele is doing well in film production since his post-quarterback career as a sports announcer ended, after American football finally got banned. He is getting yearly brain scans and diagnostic tests for the tau proteins that signal the presence of the Alzheimer's-like disease that's taken many of his teammates. Unlike the old days, now it can be treated and progression of the disease stopped if caught early. Akin is a brilliant writer for several media outlets who won his sixth Emmy last year. He and his husband have adopted a new baby girl in addition to the two boys they'd previously adopted. They can't visit Nigeria because of the new arrest-on-sight policy for gays championed by the religious leaders of the country, so Remi and Segun make the trip to New York every year to see their grandchildren.

I'm mostly quiet as everyone shares their news. After a while, Nonso gives me a searching look.

"Aisha, I ran into Iyanu at a book-signing in Otta about a month ago. She was looking good, said Ife was doing well in school. Have you heard from Okri recently?"

The rest of the group goes silent at the mention of my oldest child's name, Remi looking down and rubbing a nonexistent smudge off her shoe.

I swallow and inhale deeply to keep myself from bursting

into tears. Okri—the one person in my life with whom I have not been able to make things right. Okri inherited my smarts along with his father's stubbornness and dogged persistence. That combination has produced a long-lasting resentment of me. He was born on Thanksgiving Day in 2010. Andrew surprised me by suggesting a Nigerian name: Okri, after his favorite Nigerian writer. At first, I said, "Okri Nowak! Seriously?" The more I thought about it, though, the more I giggled. "Okay, Okri Nowak it is."

I look from Segun to Remi to Dwayne and then let my gaze settle on Nonso's face. "Okri's ex-girlfriend, you remember her, Jane, from Kansas?" They all nod; Jane has been to Nigeria many times for weddings and milestone birthday parties and, most recently, Ade's funeral, before she and Okri split up six months ago. "She called me last week. I hadn't heard from Okri, which is our usual pattern, and he hadn't returned my phone calls. This time, though, it's because he's been admitted to the top private hospital in Topeka. He'd had a lot of headaches and nausea and almost collapsed, so he was rushed to the ER. The doctors found that it was glioblastoma multiforme and he had surgery but will need further treatment. It's very aggressive. And the bill, oh my God." The tears I've been holding in begin to slide down my face.

"He's still in Kansas?" Nonso says, a look of horror slowly taking over her face. "Can he be moved to California or New York?"

I shake my head no. "The states that have universal healthcare don't allow patients from other states to just waltz in to their hospitals. He'd have to wait a year and pay a fortune before he's allowed to see any New York or California doctor. He doesn't have that kind of time."

Remi says quietly, "We should bring him home. One of my former PhD students has been working with the surgeons and oncologists at UCH. They now have machine-learning algorithms that figure out the best individualized immunotherapy for patients with aggressive tumors. They'll need his records from the Kansas hospital but they've had success even with glioblastomas." Remi got a doctorate in biomedical informatics after her sons finished middle school. Frankly, I don't understand what she does but I'll try anything that can help Okri.

I nod and say, "I already thought of bringing him home. The problem is the bill. The Kansas hospital won't release him until it's paid. His insurance covered one-tenth of the bill and then dropped him because he didn't get to the doctor to look into his headaches quickly enough. What he still owes is enough to buy a superyacht." I swipe at the tears on my face, trying to calm myself. "I've raised a third of the amount from my savings, Ade's pension, and a gift from my brother."

All eyebrows in the room go up at that. My brother and I had a falling out over my mother's wishes for her final resting place and we haven't talked to each other much in the last ten years.

Dwayne says, "We'll help out—but won't be able to chip in for another month. All our liquid assets are tied up in the academies."

I knew that already. I know my friends will help me out, but the situation is urgent. "You know Kansas passed those medical debtor laws. They won't release him until the full amount is paid," I say. I pause, sitting back in the dining chair to fully brace my spine. "Or unless . . . unless a family member takes his place."

Nonso shakes her head from side to side. "Oh God, why didn't he leave that place after Andrew died? Why did he have to stay on? His coding skills made more sense for New York or California . . ."

I make my voice as firm as possible. "That doesn't help me now Nonso. I need you and Dwayne to help bring him home. They'll release him and his records with the money I've already paid if I make it there within the next four days. I'll stay in the hospital's jail wing until I can find the rest but the most important thing is for him to get further treatment ASAP. Right now, they are just giving him post-surgery painkillers."

Remi says, "We are all coming with you to Kansas. Thank God they weren't able to strip our U.S. citizenship."

I laugh, a warm flush of relief and gratitude making me almost lightheaded. I won't have to face this alone. "Well, as long as you all leave Kansas with him and make sure he's okay in Ibadan, that's fine." I look at Dwayne and Nonso. "I'll only be locked up a month or two at the most. Who knows, maybe they'll find decent work for me since I'm a retired lawyer."

———

The flight from Ibadan to New York takes four hours on Nonso and Dwayne's Innoson HydroExcel hydrogen-hybrid jet. It's supposed to be better for the environment, as it's powered partly by batteries and releases only steam as a by-product, but I keep thinking of the Hindenburg disaster and I've almost clawed a hole into my seat's leather armrest by the time we land in JFK. We refuel and make the twenty-minute flight to an airstrip in Topeka.

At the hospital, when I finally see Okri, his mop of large, unruly curls shaven off, his face haggard, bones poking through taut skin, I hold in my breath. He is fast asleep, the pain meds keeping him in a place between hallucination and dreams. I reach for his hands and whisper his name. He opens his eyes and recoils, "No no no no, not you, not you," arms thrashing.

I feel as though a giant has knocked me flat and then decided to stomp on my belly. Repeatedly. I almost double over from the intensity of the pain. *My God, does he hate me that much? Does he even know it's me?*

"Okri," I say, my voice wobbly, ready to break, "it's Mommy. Mommy's here and everything is going to be okay." I say it the way I said it when he was three and came down with malaria

217

fever for the first time during a summer visit with my parents in Nigeria. I remember how he clung to me then, *Mommy, it hurts, make it stop,* his tiny body radiating heat like a lightbulb and all I could do when the meds fell short was wipe him down with a towel dampened in cool water and tell him that he'd be fine soon.

"Everything is going to be okay," he repeats and smiles, falling back asleep.

A weird calm comes over me then and my stomach pain subsides. I decide that he was having a nightmare when he said *No, not you.*

My friends walk me to accounts payable to get another chunk of the bill paid, thanks to Remi and Segun, and Okri's medical records sent to the University College Hospital team in Ibadan.

With the payment, we get some paperwork from the hospital to okay Okri's medical release. I've arranged for him to be flown by helicopter to the airstrip where the jet is waiting, and Remi found a Nigerian-American doctor who will accompany the flight back home and get Okri ready for the transfer to UCH.

Next, we head to another part of the hospital, get off the elevators at the sub-basement level. There's a huge set of frosted glass sliding doors across from the elevator. A large gray metal sign over the entryway reads "Restorative Work

Center." We enter into the hospital's jail. The female warden injects a microchip in my left arm, has me change into a gray jumpsuit, and hands over my civilian clothes to my waiting friends. When I am allowed back in the waiting area to say goodbye, Nonso sobs, clinging to me. "We'll have you out of here in three weeks. Just three more weeks."

"I know," I say gently. "Please make sure Okri is in treatment in Ibadan by the time I get home."

They all nod. The stupefied looks on their faces register that this is actually happening, that I'm going to be imprisoned, in spite of our position in this world.

"I'll be okay." I wave as the warden leads me to my new living quarters, through a door marked "Women's Section." Gray seems to be the theme here, for the walls, the floor, the clothing. *Abandon hope, all ye who enter*, I whisper, before forcing myself to stop. *Not helpful, Aisha. Not helpful at all.* The warden turns her head toward me and gives me a small, reassuring smile, as if she heard me. She stops outside a recessed metal door and swipes her badge. It slides open to a poorly lit room, about eleven feet by twelve feet, with a polished concrete floor. There are two twin beds set up parallel to each other at opposite ends of the room and a gray metal locker at the foot of each twin bed. She points to the bed on the left, nods, and says, "That's yours." There's no sign of the occupant of the other bed.

"Thank you," I say, my head reeling. I sway a little, suddenly frightened about being left alone in this cool, dim place. Gooseflesh sprouts on my arms.

She takes a look at my face and hers softens a little. "Cafeteria is on the second level of the hospital. Dinner starts in two hours. Here's your commissary and supplies card." She hands me a gray plastic card, pats my right hand gently as if to say *It won't be so bad*, and heads out the door. After she leaves, I put my hospital-issued toiletries and Solape's picture in the locker. Then I place pictures of Iyanu, Ife, Okri, and Ade on top of it. Seeing my family makes me feel better. As I scan the room, I bring out Solape's picture. "What do you know? Looks like we're back in boarding school," I say. She, of course, doesn't answer.

I rearrange my things in the locker and stare at the plastic card the warden handed me. I'm to use it to buy meals in the cafeteria. It has an initial balance, credit the hospital extends to all prisoners. I'll have paid it off after my first two days of work. After that, meal costs will be deducted from my pay. "I guess I won't be eating much," I say out loud.

"Oh yes you will," a voice says. "We got to enjoy something in here."

I turn around to see a stout fiftyish woman with a bad pageboy haircut and broken red veins around her nose walk into the room. I didn't hear the door open, it was so quiet. I wonder whether alcohol or something else is responsible for her bloated, puffy look.

"I'm Martha," she says, walking up to me and surprising me with a hug, when I've stuck out my hand for a shake. "My previous roommate is in the ICU for pneumonia." She gives me an accusatory look. "You're not going to do that and break my heart, are you, mama?"

Who is this woman? I think but I can't help but smile. "I don't plan to."

"Where are you from? Jamaica?"

"Oh, much more exotic than that," I say. "Roxbury, Massachusetts." I smile and wait to see how she'll react.

"Well, right on." She looks a bit puzzled.

"I have a Nigerian accent because I live in Nigeria and my dad was from there. My mom was from Roxbury though, and that's where I was born, in my grandma's house."

"I prefer hospitals myself," she says. "I picked one in St. Louis to be born. And I'm living in one now, so I guess I'm doing pretty well." She guffaws at her own joke and it rings out in a way that's infectious, so I join in.

Martha's husband died following complications from diabetes. She's been working off the debt in the hospital pharmacy for five years now, and in two more, she'll be a free woman. I tell her I'll be out in a month and she laughs again, long and hard. "Honey, that's what I said when I first came in. It's not all bad though, the work is good, you know you are helping other people get healthy."

———

I should never have married my first husband, Andrew, but at the time I thought, *He gets me better than any other man I've met, so, why not?* He tapped into a part of me that seemed to need his affirmation, his rock-solid belief in me even when I didn't believe in myself.

Andrew and I made it work for a little while after Okri was born. One day, I finally understood that I was enough for me, and it was time for me to move on with my life. Andrew had seen the end coming long before we tied the knot; he was more prepared than I was. He proposed that we live near each other so that we could share joint custody of our son, and we were fine in Chicago for a while. Until the election of 2016.

There were many, many beginnings but I guess you could say the final unhinging began when a brilliant sociopath whose country had fallen from its once lofty perch took a deeper look at the dark underside of U.S. history: smallpox on blankets; vast economic power forged from whips, cotton, and the misery of bondage; men selling their half-white children born of rape to other men for profit; the annexation of dusky-hued kingdoms; the Japanese internment camps; glorification of corporate greed over humanity. From half a world away, he recognized the deep resentment and persistent fear of retribution that consumed many after the 2008 and 2012 elections. He realized something that had occurred to none of his country's previous rulers. There was no need for guns, grenades, bombs, tanks, no need for armed, fidgety young men in tight-fitting uniforms lined up as far as the eye could see, for drones or robotic warriors. There was a core group of Americans who would do all the work for him with the hate they carried in their hearts and a charismatic narcissist he'd met several times itching to lead them. The propaganda channels already existed, ready to be weaponized. It worked very well.

Ade and I had gotten married in Chicago in 2014, two years after my divorce. We all got along and I was happy that Okri had two men he could call his father. Andrew, Okri, Ade, and I moved to California in January 2017, seven months before Iyanu was born. By 2021, we had a newly elected nativist government, which won the electoral college in spite of losing the popular vote by 8 million. The new president declared that naturalized Americans from countries with GDPs of less than a trillion dollars had nothing to offer "real Americans" and would be stripped of their U.S. citizenship. Exceptions would be made on a case-by-case basis for those with documented European heritage. Ade and I decided to join the exodus. Andrew was angry with us, said we were taking the coward's way out, said we should stand and fight, that I, of all people, should fight because I had roots in the U.S.

deeper than his, deeper even than the head of the neofascist movement. I tried to explain to him that I love the U.S. but I have always loved Nigeria too, that I had thought about moving back as far back as 2015, when Remi and Segun joined Nonso and Dwayne there. I said I would take the best part of America with me wherever I went but I was tired of fighting this particular fight and there were other fights in other places worthy of my attention. He looked so disappointed.

I remember grabbing his hand then and saying, "Andrew, listen to me. I feel like I've been living on a roller coaster since 2016, moving from depression to anger to fear to action and back again. In 2017, I tipped over from a mildly elevated blood pressure that my doctor was optimistic about into full-blown stage-two hypertension, even with meds. I can't sleep, I'm suspicious of both people I know and people I don't know, and some days I lie in bed paralyzed and think that I'm about to have a stroke. I've marched, I've voted, I've petitioned, I've written postcards, phone-banked, I've donated to every sane candidate and organization there is, I've cried on the phone thanking my representatives for their votes, I've memorized zip codes in red states so I can phone congresspeople that I think have lost their minds. I've lost faith in half of my country. I just can't live like this anymore. Not even in California. I. Just. Can't. Do. This. Anymore."

Andrew looked stunned for a minute. Then he nodded his head yes. He said, "Aisha, I hear you. I get it. I want you to know that I've joined messengerRNA. I had to. For Okri. I have to stay here and I want him to stay with me."

I shook my head no and he said, "Aisha, we're in Los Angeles, a majority-minority city. California is leading the resistance. I'll take care of him. He'll be safe."

———

In 2018, Racism is Not American or RNA was formed by a multiethnic coalition aghast at what the U.S. was becoming. They held huge rallies in coastal and midwestern cities, put up billboards and ads decrying the decline of the country, and declared themselves a peaceful resistance movement. The newsmedia largely ignored them because, let's face it, peaceful resistance really isn't sexy and bores most people to tears. The majority of the U.S. population continued to move to coastal cities, leaving the vast interior to the nativists, who understood the power of two senators and the electoral college in ways that their adversaries didn't seem to grasp fully.

MessengerRNA, or mRNA, was an offshoot of RNA: a smaller group of white fathers of non-white children who were determined to fight for their children's place in this new constitutionally enshrined landscape of permanent minority rule. They devoured the writings of Robin DiAngelo, Tim Wise, Michelle Alexander, Bryan Stevenson, Isabel Wilkerson, and Nancy MacLean. They alternately flirted with and were repulsed by certain ideas from anarchists. They weren't sure that nonviolent protest was going to be effective this time around but, to a man, they would have keeled over at the sight of blood.

After a long-drawn-out argument in which I suggested he might not dislike living in Nigeria as much as he thought, Andrew and I agreed that Okri would live with him but visit me and Ade and his sister every summer. Andrew promised that they would stick to coastal cities, because the interior was no place for a young black boy. I gave in because of his complete devotion to Okri, because he hadn't moved on, didn't have anyone else, would have been devastated to lose Okri. I gave in because a tiny voice inside me wondered whether things would be a little bit easier with just me, Ade, and Iyanu. I listened to that voice. I listened and only Okri can forgive me but he won't. In December 2021, Ade, Iyanu, and I boarded a plane for Nigeria and left our home in California behind.

By late 2022, RNA and the ACLU had teamed up to end the nativists' citizenship-stripping plans. They filed lawsuit after lawsuit and won every court case. More than a million U.S. citizens, including Ade and me, had already left the country. Since my mother was African-American and Ade was born in Oakland, we were never actually in direct danger of losing our citizenship, but with nativists emboldened post-election in ways we had never seen before, we'd decided that it would be better to raise our family in a less hostile environment. After RNA and the ACLU's court victories, only 100,000 departed citizens returned to the U.S., most of us having elected to be dual citizens living overseas, denouncing the nativists safely from a distance. Smarting from its losses in court, the unpopular U.S. administration decided that the best way to distract the public and gin up fresh domestic support was to start a new, easily winnable war with Venezuela.

Beginning in 2022, Okri summered with us yearly in Nigeria. The summer of 2024, he arrived in June and we started as we usually did, with a tour of his favorite places: we found a small hotel near the blue waters of Lake Oguta, savoring hot peppersoup with chunks of fresh fish plucked from its waters daily. I was amused by Okri's insistence on eating this every afternoon, even as he sniffled, nose dripping, face contorted with that peculiar combination of discomfort and delight common to scotch bonnet pepper aficionados. Next, we visited the Obudu Mountain Resort, then took in the sculpted walls and greenery of the Osun Sacred Grove, and finally flew north to see the ancient Kano City Walls and visit Yankari National Park. Iyanu followed her big brother around like a lost puppy and I was moved at how he never brushed her aside, always found time for her even when he must have felt irritated by her clinginess. Then Remi called three weeks before Okri was to head back to California, Andrew, and school, asking whether I'd seen the BBC World News breaking broadcast, her voice almost cracking.

That's how I found out. A messengerRNA group, frustrated

with a lack of progress in the Senate on vital issues, had decided to hold certain members of Congress hostage. A group of ten had managed to get into the chamber with undetectable plastic polymer guns. Which were unloaded but security had no way of knowing that until a sniper took out the ringleader and the others surrendered. Andrew was with that mRNA group. He initially got twenty years out of a possible thirty because none of the guns were loaded. In 2026, with help from friends of ours who were lawyers, he received a reduced sentence of eighteen years for his role in the operation. Okri was sixteen years old when this happened.

Andrew was sentenced to prison in Leavenworth, Kansas, so Kansas is where Okri decided to go to college once he turned eighteen and I no longer had the legal right to keep him in Nigeria. He visited his father every week until Andrew died from a stroke fifteen years into his sentence. By then Okri was so consumed with anger and misery, he'd decided that I was the reason his father ended up in jail. If I had loved Andrew as much as he loved me, if I had given him a chance, Okri told me at the funeral, Andrew wouldn't have joined messengerRNA's mission on that day. His words rankled but I felt his grief and knew better than to try to argue with him.

My first seven days in the debtor's prison have been relatively uneventful. The women's section seems to be run by the warden and a square-jawed guard whose looks mask the fact that she is a soft-hearted pushover once you get to know her. I've received my daily schedule, which is to work in accounts payable, checking numbers on spreadsheets and flagging accounts with balances that are overdue for further review. Martha has been assigned to show me around the first week, which she loves because it's a break from the monotony of her job counting pills in the pharmacy. I get a ninety-minute break after lunch just by myself back in our shared room. Martha thinks it's on account of my age. We eat at the hospital cafeteria with everyone else; staff, visitors, nurses, doctors, and the only thing that sets us apart is our gray uniforms. I'm puzzled by the seeming lack of security. What's to stop me from just walking out the door during work hours and disappearing?

My ninth evening, after a dinner of disgusting sloppy-joe-look-alike mush, I ask Martha, "How come no one just walks away during the day? There doesn't seem to be any guard really watching us."

Her eyes narrow and get really serious. "I knew a guy who tried that once. He worked in the pharmacy too. Somehow got ahold of regular clothes, changed, and walked out the door just like the visitors. Made it through the hospital gates and kept walking toward downtown. Then he says he collapsed in a heap on the sidewalk. His muscles wouldn't work, he was drooling and peed himself, and they just left him there for hours, even after people walking by called nine-one-one. When they were ready, the hospital sent people to scoop him up. After that, he wouldn't even go out to walk around the hospital garden like we all do."

My mouth was agape. "What . . . ? How . . . ?"

"That chip in your arm has a tracker," she said. "And it has something else too. When you walk beyond a certain distance from the hospital boundary it kicks in something. Like a muscle relaxant that would fell an elephant. Trust me, honey, you don't want to mess with that. It doesn't kick in on the grounds or even by the gate but walk beyond that and hoo boy."

"So . . . no one has ever escaped?"

"I heard that someone else tried. Before I got locked up. Don't know whether the story is true, but they say he got to downtown and then the muscle relaxer thing kicked in but this time it was at night. And some crazies thought it would be the most hilarious thing to set him on fire just for the fun of it. The hospital scooped up his body hours later and his daughter had to take his place because the debt wasn't paid off yet."

"A funeral and another family member locked up," I say. My stomach begins to roil.

Later that night, I'm awakened by a muffled sound. I lie on my back and listen. It's exactly what I thought it was. I swing my feet over the side of the twin bed, stand, and almost fall as a stabbing pain shoots through my right ankle. My joints seem to bother me here in a way they never did in Nigeria. I think it's the coolness, the damp chill of the room. It gets into my bones. I ignore the pain and hobble over to Martha's bed.

"Martha," I say.

She weeps even louder now, the thin coverlet quivering beneath my fingers. "I'm sorry, I just can't stop." She shudders and gasps as I sit on the edge of her bed.

"What's wrong, Martha?"

"Today's my daughter's eighteenth birthday. It's the fifth birthday I've missed in here and now she's a woman. By the time I get out of here she'll probably be married with a kid. She'll have no use for me." She sits up suddenly, grips me in a bear hug, and wails.

I hold her tight and make shushing sounds, even as my arms begin to feel sore. "I'm sure your daughter loves you and she'll want her kids to know their grandma," I say.

Martha calms down. "You're probably right. It . . . It just kills me that I missed so many things, you know? Her first period. When she got bullied in school because I was in here. Those knuckleheads think they'll always be healthy. That their parents will always be healthy. When my mom told me, I wanted so bad to go to her school and shove some kids into a wall . . ."

"We'll celebrate her birthday today with cake from the cafeteria," I say, trying to distract her. "It's on me."

Martha sniffles and sighs. "You don't have to do that."

"I want to," I say. "I haven't had cake in a long time. Go back to sleep."

She lies back down but holds on to my hand. I sit there until her breathing gets shallow and even, then I make my way gingerly back to my bed, favoring my left foot.

It's three a.m. but I know I'm done with sleep. My feet, arms, and shoulders ache. I lie back and think about my life, think about Martha and her daughter, all the Marthas in this sub-basement, far away from their loved ones.

I think about my recent conversations with Iyanu and Ife. They call me every day when I'm on break, though it's late at night in Nigeria. Iyanu tells me that Okri is already responding to the immunotherapy at UCH and I don't know whether she's saying that to make me feel better or if it's really true. My conversations with Ife have been eye-opening. My granddaughter has decided that it's okay to carry on a conversation with me that has no mention of religion. She has an acerbic sense of humor about current events that I've never heard her express before, and while I enjoy this new (to me) display of cutting wit, it occurs to me that her faith is the only thing keeping her from collapsing into a volcanic ash heap of despair. I have been unfair to Ife. There's a lot going on in that head of hers.

I drift off a little and that's when I see Solape walking toward me with Okri, a gaunt, thin Okri who kneels before me with several constellations mapped on his shaven scalp. Solape points and raises her right arm and the stars on his scalp brighten and rise, taking their place above us. There's Polaris, Regulus, Antares, Canopus, and Sirius. I see the constellations Orion, Aquarius, and Andromeda levitate, followed by Cassiopeia. Next, the seven stars of the Plough take flight and then his scalp is free of illumination and Okri smiles, the way he used to when he was two and Andrew and I and he made up the known universe. I thank Solape but she turns away from me, shaking her head. I feel it then, the python squeezing, squeezing, and I gasp for breath. I wonder whether this is how Solape felt the night she died, her lungs screaming for her inhaler, for anything that makes that life-giving air flow. But she had asthma. I've never had asthma. I try to say Solape's name but I can't speak, can't move. I start to shiver, I feel so cold and then I realize that right now, I have the silence I have always craved, no voices in my head, least of all mine, chastising me for the things I could have done, the things I could have said, the things I could have been. I gasp again and I say *thank you*. I get the words out, *thank you*, to Nonso and Remi, to Andrew and Ade and Okri and Iyanu and Ife. *Thank you*, because now, now I truly see, within the silence, this silence, I can finally be.

ACKNOWLEDGMENTS

This book has been almost a decade and a half in the making, in time manufactured after writing, rewriting, and executing research grants; submitting and revising journal articles; learning new programming languages and machine learning techniques; creating informatics syllabi; and teaching.

I would like to thank all those who have helped me sharpen my writing along the way, especially Chika Unigwe, Molara Wood, Muthoni Garland, and Petina Gappah on Zoetrope in the early aughts; Ellen Litman and Ian Breen of Grub Street, Boston; as well as Edan Lepucki and Ivy Pochoda in different Los Angeles workshops. Ivy, thank you for your support, your generosity with your time, and for introducing me to Jen Pooley.

Thanks to Molara Wood for my first published story, an early version of "Fodo's Better Half," in a 2007 issue of *Farafina*.

To my writing group—Bill Loving, Laura Gold, and Charles Webb, thank you for your invaluable critiques, company, scrumptious fare in pre–COVID-19 times, and willingness to adapt to Zoom in the COVID-19 era.

I am grateful to my brother Dayo for badgering me to submit a story to a PEN competition in South Africa and refusing to be ignored until I gave in, exasperated. Having "Area Boy Rescue" selected as a finalist in that competition made me start to believe that I had it in me to finish writing a book. Dayo was the coauthor of my first book attempt at age eight, a mess that included car chases, explosions, and tea parties, and ended in ripped pages and tears due to our "creative differences."

Isi Okogun, my personal person, thank you so much for your help with "Area Boy Rescue."

My everlasting gratitude to my freelance editor, Jenn Pooley, who declared that she would be my "fairy godmother" and summoned a literary agent from the ether when the first agent who made me a contract offer suddenly balked.

Thanks to Mollie Glick for seeing the potential in a collection of stories with recurring characters, getting me to write a few more, and being the best agent that a person could ask for.

To Patrik Henry Bass, thank you for getting this book, with its jigsaw puzzle quirks and for helping me to fashion it into a novel in stories. Thanks also to Francesca Walker and the entire team at Amistad/HarperCollins.

Thanks to my husband Alejandro, for reading and critiquing countless drafts of each story and being the greatest cheerleader for my work.

Thanks to my mother Chikwenye, for the hundreds of amazing books that surrounded me growing up in Ibadan, books that set my imagination on fire and served both as a refuge from household chores and an inexpensive vacation around the world (and sometimes into space). Once I'd read pretty much every book in the house, thank you for taking me to the University of Ibadan Bookshop and the Abadina Children's Library, and later, for the gift of travel around Nigeria and to a variety of African countries. I am truly grateful for your help with research on "Fodo's Better Half."

Dulcie Kermah, I truly appreciate your help with research for "Guardian Angel of Elmina."

Uzo Iweala, thank you for your advice and words of wisdom on the publishing process.

For expanding my literary horizons at Barnard and for great conversations about Buchi Emecheta, thank you Professor Quandra Prettyman. Rest in peace.

To my FGGC Oyo sisters, thank you for your friendship and for teaching me how to be independent at a young age. Thank you to the Federal Government of Nigeria for subsidizing my secondary school education, which exposed me to books by a variety of African authors and to Richard Wright's *Native Son*.

Thank you to all the literary magazines, big and small,

thriving and defunct, that give emerging writers a chance to break through. Thanks in particular to *Farafina*, *Camera Obscura Journal of Literature and Photography*, and *Ploughshares* for publishing my stories.

Octavia Butler, thank you for being well ahead of your time and showing so many writers a way forward through an understanding of history.

Awon omo UI, too many to mention, it was wonderful and a privilege growing up with you in that bubble, a source of delightful memories and lasting inspiration for me.

Last, but not least, to the taxpayers of the Commonwealth of Massachusetts, thank you for funding the Boston Public Library, Copley Square, where the first drafts of most of the stories in this book were written.

ABOUT THE AUTHOR

Omolola Ijeoma Ogunyemi was born and raised in Ibadan, Nigeria. A finalist for the 2009 PEN/Studzinski Literary Award, her stories and poetry have appeared in *New Writing from Africa 2009*, *Ploughshares*, *The Massachusetts Review*, the *Indiana Review*, *Wasafiri*, *Dance the Guns to Silence: 100 Poems for Ken Saro-Wiwa*, and *The American Poetry Review*. She graduated from Barnard and UPenn with bachelor's, master's, and doctoral degrees in computer science. Omolola is a professor of preventive and social medicine at Charles R. Drew University of Medicine and Science in South Los Angeles, where she teaches and conducts research on using biomedical informatics to reduce health disparities. She lives in Los Angeles with her husband.